RADICAL PRUNINGS

RADICAL PRUNINGS

A NOVEL OF OFFICIOUS ADVICE
FROM THE CONTESSA OF COMPOST

BONNIE THOMAS ABBOTT

emmis
books

For further information, contact the publisher at:
Emmis Books
The Old Firehouse
1700 Madison Ave.
Cincinnati, OH 45206
www.emmisbooks.com

Library of Congress Cataloging-in-Publication Data

Abbott, Bonnie Thomas, 1942-
    Radical prunings : a novel of officious advice from the contessa of compost
/ by Bonnie Thomas Abbott.
    p. cm.
  ISBN-13: 978-1-57860-203-2
  ISBN-10: 1-57860-203-3
  1. Gardening--Humor.   I. Title.
  PN6231.G3A23 2005
  814'.6--dc22

2005011715

Edited by Michael J. Rosen
Interior designed by Greg Hischak
Cover designed by Carie Adams

Distributed by Publishers Group West

For Raymonde

—her hollyhocks became my ballerinas

ACKNOWLEDGMENTS

With gratitude to Michael J. Rosen for a quarter-century of friendship and encouragement.

Earlier versions of material from this book previously appeared in *Mirth of a Nation: The Best Contemporary Humor* (HarperCollins, 2000) and *Seattle Weekly.*

RADICAL PRUNINGS

Foreword

DON'T BE AFRAID TO ASK

On Open Day, the general public, often for a small donation to charity, is allowed to traipse through private gardens and gawk at the product of genuine obsession. On Open Day, I place a sign by my gate which reads: DON'T BE AFRAID TO ASK.

I seem to have unjustly acquired a reputation for being a bit formidable. Newcomers often hesitate to approach me with their questions, so I will embolden them by asking a few questions of myself:

Q: Why would I expend all the trouble and treasure, beginning weeks in advance of Open Day, just to submit my private passion to the curiosity of strangers?

A: Because we gardeners are exhibitionists. The first thing we do when our friends come to call is show off our gardens, pointing out every new acquisition (we are shamelessly acquisitive), not leaving out any details about price and the difficulty of the pursuit. And if we know our friends well enough, we inspect their gardens before we even ring the doorbell. There's no triumph in getting all dolled up in a new frock just to spend the evening alone.

❧❧❧

Q: What kind of people come to Open Day?

A: All kinds of people come through:

- Gardening friends who volunteer to answer visitors' questions and stay for dinner afterwards
- New homeowners looking for ideas
- Lonely people who want to engage a fellow gardener in a conversation
- Neighbors' cats who have decided that the cool seclusion of an oakleaf hydrangea near the bird feeder is worth risking discovery by my dogs
- Snoopy people who try to see inside the house
- Garden journalists, including one who views any changes since he left as indication of contemptible neglect and pathetic decline
- People just passing by who need to use a bathroom
- Even a Dutchman on a bicycle

Q: What can I learn on Open Day?

A: Visitors tell me that if this were their garden, they would just sit and look at it for hours. Well, I do. But what they must learn is that a landscaping company truck didn't just pull up one day and a crew of college students didn't just spill out, with a machine ripping up this and smoothing that, a bag of this scattered and a barrel of that sprayed, holes drilled and flowers and shrubs plugged in like hair transplants and presto—at the end of the day, a garden. No. What I will tell them is that this is a project that has been refined and revised, day by day, year by year, over decades, and that there have been plenty of disappointments and devastations, money down the drain, cut and bit throbbing fingers and slivers and thorns dug out, hot compresses and ice packs, and orthopedic repair to get to all this loveliness.

Now that you've got up your courage, if you're baffled by a plant you can't identify, or wonder why a specimen in the host's garden looks so much better than yours, or why you never seem to come up with combinations or compositions as attractive as the host's, just ask. There's a good chance that the host has a whole nursery bed of potted-up seedlings and rooted cuttings that she can't bear to throw onto the compost heap, so if you wish you had a seedpod or a cutting from one of the host's plants (no pinching of your own allowed), just ask.

Come through my gate and enjoy your visit. And if you have questions, DON'T BE AFRAID TO ASK. It's Open Day.

RADICAL PRUNINGS

Gardening Advice by Mertensia Corydalis

INTO THE GARDEN

"Something with leaves and tendrils," was my uncharacteristically vague description of what I wanted, as though the sculptor could read my mind. That's what I tell visitors to my garden who ask about the rather unusual, massive (in the scale of the sculptor, who is nearly seven feet tall) gate through which they must pass. I must have imagined that the sculptor shared my vision of a rapturously filigreed Paris Metro type of entrance. I can draw well enough that I could have given him a fair representation of how I saw it, and no artist working in black iron would have been in doubt for a moment if I had just said the words: "Art Nouveau." After a month of impatient waiting, a mufflerless, psychedelically decorated truck delivered the completed gate and a crew to install it. It was not at all what I had wanted. It was better.

Made of recycled scrap iron, in the spirit of allowing nothing to go to waste in an organically maintained garden, the asymmetrical gate parts in the middle. One side is a flourish of leaves, as sturdy and sharp as garden implements, and fat tendrils (the sculptor took care to learn that all the tendrils of a plant curl in the same direction). The other side represents a thicket of bare twigs, bluntly cut from their winter dormant pruning, but with the swelling of buds along their length. And that is the life of a garden.

Over the years, visitors to my garden columns in *Cutting Borders Magazine,* in my newsletter, and, most recently, on the Internet have inquired about a compilation. There have been hundreds of columns, thousands of letters with questions from readers. There have been letters from trophy gardeners, the sort who just had transplanted onto their property a mighty oak on which John Quincy Adams once relieved himself. Now they want a little advice on upkeep. What they really want is an announcement in my column about this incredible acquisition.

Beginners' letters are my favorites. The writers could have gotten their answers more quickly from other sources by the time I receive their query and the answer is published, but what they really want is to have their hand held by an experienced gardener. They want someone to tell them that if they made a mistake with a new plant purchase, it's all right to dig it up and find a better home for it (even if that means the compost heap), or if a favorite plant eventually dies, it's not the end of the world. Plant life is renewable. There's another specimen out there waiting to be lavished with your love and attention.

My garden gate cost me a fat check, more than I really could afford at the time, and a sports car which the young sculptor fancied. The car had been bought as impractical but flashy transportation for a newly single mother, who found it necessary to put the convertible top down in order to transport bales of straw and burlap-balled saplings, even as the snow still flew in early March. Over time, the car had been retired to the garage, too expensive to insure with a teenage driver in the household, too unreliable even for a quick trip to the market, too much the source of college tuition payments for my mechanic's children.

The sculptor brought his mechanic along when it was time to collect the sports car. Some magic went on under the bonnet, and the engine, which had not turned over in many years, coughed in hesitation, then exploded to life. The sculptor threw back the top, slid the seat all the way back to accommodate his very long legs, and backed the car down the driveway. I felt a sudden panic on hearing again the engine's throaty gurgle. I heard it shifted up to highway speed, then gone out of earshot, that part of my life. I turned to my beautiful new gate. It is solid. It has gravity. It and the garden beyond it are here to stay.

No matter whether the portal to the garden is your kitchen door or a fancy gate, what lies beyond is your personal vision of paradise, a paradise that is a perpetual work in progress. In my gardening advice columns, my mission is to offer a little guidance and a glimpse into my own paradise in progress. In this book, then, I present you with a selection of two years' worth of my newsletters. Welcome to my garden.

—*Mertensia Corydalis*

SPRING

In the Spring, the Stork brings baby bunnies to the cabbage patch

THE CHILD

cities but with no hatred of each other

wound for a gr

with the torn remaining

shou.ders. William had brought him in an

for a rabbit for the usual rules shown oppose

you can kind of control abuses all plant tomatoes in wa

loved the old man and often want to see him. So did Lucy

...ickly now. In only a week, they have de

...nd tiny claws and teeth. By now, they ca

...ks. Very soon their bright, brown eyes

RADICAL PRUNINGS

MARCH 10

Gardening Advice by Mertensia Corydalis

WHOSE GARDEN IS IT, ANYWAY?

Dear Readers,

It has been a glorious day! Tran has returned to us full time from his winter position at the Metro Botanical Conservatory.

The morning began with a rendezvous in my garden, gently pulling away the blankets of compost, straw, chopped leaves, and hardwood chips, to reveal blanched but determined tips of leaves and stems, both of us making notes.

What a joy it is to perch beside him on a wooden stool in the still-chilly potting shed, sketching ideas, making shopping lists, knowing that his calm face and strong hands will be just steps away from my door.

Returning to my library/office, I see, from the stack of letters and e-mail printouts that my secretary Miss Vong has arranged on my desk, that you are like racehorses kicking at their stalls, eager to get outside and churn up some dirt. We will start with a few questions that represent the concerns of many of our readers.

Q: Dear Mertensia, a few warm days woke up my crocus. The leaves are well out of the ground. What will happen if the weather turns cold again? Will the flowers be ruined? Is there anything I can do? What about the bulbs—will they be damaged? —*Agnes, Lambdon*

A: Dear Agnes, looking now at the snow-crusted crocus in my own garden, I cannot forget the very day their progenitors were planted. I crawled around on hands and knees for hours one October day nearly thirty years ago, making hundreds of holes with a dibble, while my daughter Astrid toddled along after me, placing a crocus bulb in each hole ("Pointy end up, angel, hairy end down, like Daddy"). Norton, my former husband, who had taken to wearing Japanese farmer pants buttoned at the ankles; clogs which never needed hosing off, since he never stepped off the pea-gravel paths; and a straw coolie hat with chin cord which could be pushed back to hang behind his shoulders if he ever happened to work up a sweat, walked up and down the edge of the bed pointing with a bamboo switch, "There. And there. And there." I wondered what it would feel like to plunge a fat dibble into the flesh of a human foot.

Returning to your questions, Agnes, early spring-flowering bulbs are more often than not caught up in the cruel tantrums of late winter and sometimes the blooms are shredded by an ice storm or reduced to mush by a hard freeze, but the bulbs survive, leaving hope for the following year. Fortunately most years the blooms overcome adversity (it's in the breeding). Your questions tell me you are a new gardener, so I will give you a bit more advice. Always give yourself permission to rearrange or remove whatever displeases you in your own garden.

؟🔊؟🔊؟🔊

Q: Dear Miss Corydalis, three years ago I planted a one-gallon pot of zebra grass close to a tiny pond. Now it is about six times larger in circumference and looks out of proportion in its location. I want to transplant it, but can't seem to dig it up with a sharp spade. Last year, I tried chopping at the roots with a hatchet and, as a last resort, cut it back and sprayed it with an herbicide. (It sent up new growth immediately!) Help! —*Wiley, Savage Flats*

A: Dear Wiley, normally I would hit the roof seeing the word "herbicide" in my mailbag, but I understand your desperation. I know that bone-jarring feeling when you hit the stolons, as unyielding as steel cables, with your spade. Your teeth are probably still vibrating. You have about as much hope of budging this clump as you do of killing a vampire with a plastic fork.

Let this be a little Sunday-school lesson for the rest of the readers—before you plant that innocent-looking gallon-size clump of ornamental grass, think long and hard about the location. And if the grass in question is a running type with fast-spreading underground stolons, such as many varieties of bamboo, the plant will go off on its merry way if you are not careful, and soon be thumbing its nose at you from your neighbor's yard. The only advice I have to offer our friend Wiley is to hire a professional tree-removal company to dig out the clump, or, if you're on a budget, detonate a do-it-yourself thermonuclear device.

Q. Miss Mertensia, I live in an exclusive housing development which requires that the homeowners use the services of a chemical lawn-treatment company. The more I read about the benefits of organic gardening, the more disturbed I am about having the lawn treated chemically. The front lawns here are immense, and ground covers are only permitted under trees, and then only in a five-foot radius from the base of the trunk. Only one tree per quarter acre of lawn is allowed, and the trees must be approved in advance by the homeowners' association so that they are placed to present a uniform pattern when viewed from the private aircraft of the more prominent members of the community. So you see, I am kind of boxed in on this issue. Please suggest some organic substitutes which will make the lawn green enough to pass the monthly spectrogram test administered by the village police. What is your advice? —*Lawrence, Battersby Village*

A. Dear Lawrence, here is my advice: Put the house up for sale immediately before your soul is sucked out through your nasal passages. Run. Save yourself.

Miss Vong has her instructions for the season: lawn questions go into a separate pile, to be addressed after I attend a night class on quantum mechanics. Or better yet, send those questions to my replacement in the editorial offices at *Cutting Borders Magazine*.

Next time ... ridding your garden of gnawing, boring insects

RADICAL PRUNINGS

MARCH 16

Gardening Advice by Mertensia Corydalis

NOTHING RHYMES WITH ORANGE

Dear Readers,

If your Miss Mertensia is a bit peevish as we write this newsletter, it may be because the Mulchmeister Company driver just dumped a truckload of mulch in the middle of my driveway, blocking my garage and causing me to miss an important meeting with my publisher. On top of that, it was cypress mulch, not hardwood, as ordered. Tran has been on the kitchen telephone demanding immediate removal of the cypress and unloading of the correct replacement. When I took a break to fetch a cup of coffee, Tran was searching the inside of my refrigerator as he waited on hold. I heard a soda can popped open. "I am tearing up your invoice at this moment," he told someone. "Let me speak with Nancy."

Speaking with whoever Nancy is seems to require speaking to her *sotto voce* in the privacy of the refrigerator door while I am still in the kitchen. A load of the correct mulch appeared within the hour.

I see from your letters that you are in a buying mood, and

that will make the nurserymen very happy indeed. I have to confess, your Miss Mertensia is now making almost-daily visits to the garden centers to see if something new has arrived, if nothing but baskets of pansies and primroses in comic book colors. On to a few of your letters:

Q. I have a shady area that is dark and boring. How about planting impatiens to add a little color? What is the lowest light intensity for impatiens to bloom? —*Willard, Westbrook*

A. Willard, I see that you do not live in South Africa, so why would you imply to the viewer that these gaudy, waterlogged pathetic little flowers just happened to land in some dismal corner of your yard, only to become compost at the first breath of light frost? Muster your powers of observation, if you have any, and notice that the understory of trees is dappled with light. Choose hardy native plants, such as pulmonaria, whose white-spotted foliage will light up the darkest corner and bloom with lovely blue and pink flowers in April. By the way, what is throwing this shade in the first place? I suppose it is some hideous aluminum hut housing your riding lawn mower.

❧❧❧❧

Q. I'm new to gardening and want to try my hand at roses. I recall a bright orange one my parents were particularly proud of called Tropicana. Should I buy one potted or bare-root? —*Lois, Dudley*

A. Lois, Lois. Where is your brain? Why in the world would you crave a rose the color of a vinyl couch in the waiting room of your local muffler shop? Color aside, as a novice to rose growing, you have no business tossing your money away on temperamental hybrid teas. Instead, investigate sturdy shrub roses. They only come in pastels and muted reds. They will serve you well until you develop some sense of color and knowledge of rose cultivation.

❧❧❧

Q. Last fall I lifted my canna bulbs and stored them in the unheated pool house. It did not get too cold this winter. Do you think the bulbs will be okay to plant again this year? —*Chad, New Leicester*

A. What a pity! All that money and no taste. Do you live in the Yucatan Peninsula? I thought not. Then why are you growing tropical plants with big hot-colored blooms in the middle of what was formerly prime farmland? Refer to Questions No. 1 and 2 in today's column. Throw the damn things out and collect rare, dwarf conifers. You can afford it.

❧❧❧

Q. We just bought a new home and are confused by all the lawn-care companies' spraying programs. Is it necessary to spray for grubs? —*Tim and Courtney, Sycamore Grove*

A. Have you noticed that the lawn-chemical companies put a teeny sign on your lawn when they are done? It has a picture of a child and a dog with a slash through them.

You don't even have to read to understand the sign. It means that a couple of years from now, after your pet has licked this poison off its bare feet every day, you will spend about a thousand dollars for futile chemotherapy treatments at the veterinary hospital. It will take a little longer to affect your children since they probably don't play outdoors in bare feet, being driven to all their pressing recreational appointments in their mother's mini van.

Moreover, I don't appreciate breathing the vapors and drinking the lawn chemicals that have run off into the local river on their way downtown to the water-treatment facility, all so people like you can try to emulate the sweeping grassy vistas of the Palais de Versailles in front of your Heritage Craftsman Home. This is the last lawn-care question I will entertain—ever.

GLEANINGS

Impatient, I Presume: The first collected specimens of impatiens were taken to England by a member of one of Dr. David Livingstone's expeditions. The plant promptly escaped and became a worldwide suburban menace.

What was essentially a colorful weed, the wild impatiens caught the eye of Claude Hope, an American military officer assigned to Costa Rica during World War II. He stayed on, and breeding impatiens became his life's work. The successor to Hope's flower farm, Linda Vista, is now the world's foremost producer of impatien seeds, from which all those millions of flats are grown.

As a gardener and designer of gardens, I have never been a fan of "instant color." Gardening is all about patience. Like writing a definitive book on *Pulmonaria*, some things just can't be rushed.

Next time ... on growing zucchini ... composting pet waste ... gazing balls

RADICAL PRUNINGS

MARCH 21

Gardening Advice by Mertensia Corydalis

HOAX, BUGS, AND ROCK AND ROLL

Dear Readers,

Our newsletter is a little late this time, as my accountant, Ms. Marvell, is driving poor Miss Vong and me to distraction, questioning every receipt and cancelled check for tax time. How can one possibly explain what one spent during the year on the garden? And then there was the small investment in my brother Artur's latest entrepreneurial venture, e-Mobius. Artie assured me that all the large corporations are, as his prospectus presented it, "outsourcing front office horizontal uplinkage." Unfortunately, there has been a vertical downlinkage, causing landscaping plans shrinkage here at Miltonhurst.

To help support our own spring garden, we have taken on a major design project, the refurbishing of the estate garden of a certain music star who aspires to lead the life of a country squire in his advancing years. I know you are all burning with curiosity, but Miss Mertensia would never compromise the privacy of her clients. But here is a little hint: think of a popular Tyrolean smoked cheese. The project will be quite a challenge. We have already had several incoherent telephone conversations regarding the project, followed by a wobbly stroll through a small part of the garden (all he could manage, it being still daylight) accompanied by a stern-looking nurse who was there to give the Big Cheese his afternoon enema when the walk was done.

When Miss Vong learned that Tran, my garden assistant, would be accompanying me to chart the present layout and take soil samples, Miss Vong insisted that she come along to help make notes. She claims to know some form of Vietnamese shorthand, although this is the first I've learned that she possesses this skill. Besides, she pointed out, I would be depriving her of the opportunity to meet someone famous (apparently I don't count).

Miss Vong, steno pad ready, came dressed in elasticized Capri pants and her Phat Maudit World Tour T-shirt, not appropriate garden-business attire as far as I'm concerned, but who listens to my opinions in this organization? Miss Vong soon tired of trying to keep up with us in her platform shoes and went off in search of refreshment. She turned up, all aglow, as we concluded our survey. Apparently the Teutonically handsome Herr Rubric, Chef to the Stars, gave her a tour of the state-of-the-art kitchen, showing off his industrial-size reach-in cooler.

The garden is in a shabby state of neglect, with walkway pavers heaved, out-of-shape shrubbery and box hedges, a fetid algae lagoon, party glassware and empty bottles under every bush and amidst every ground cover, and a Roman bath's worth of statuary of nymphs and naiads and muscular deities, all spray-painted with offensive graffiti. I could see members of the grounds staff crouched behind a pair of yews, watching our inspection party. They should be very, very afraid.

We will update you on this project from time to time.

Q. Dear Mertensia, my bearded iris had a lot of foliage but failed to bloom last summer. Could the problem be thrips?
—*Alistair, Hamford*

A. "Alistair," don't even bother inspecting and dusting for thrips. I could see from my yard when you, the know-it-all, planted the rhizomes so deep that half the length of the leaves were covered by soil. If you lived to be a hundred, as will the iris, they would never bloom. Notice that when iris multiplies on its own, the rhizomes are right at the surface. Now what does that tell you? More's the pity, as you will never enjoy the flowers' subtle fragrance of Grapette soda; the fleshy, erect curve of the standards; the saffron-hued brush at the base of each languidly draping fall. But then, I notice you never have any visitors besides your mother.

❧❧❧

Next time ... aren't you sorry you didn't plant more hyacinths?

MARCH

APRIL

MAY

JUNE

JULY

AUGUST

SEPTEMBER

OCTOBER

NOVEMBER

DECEMBER

JANUARY

FEBRUARY

RADICAL PRUNINGS

MARCH 29

Gardening Advice by Mertensia Corydalis

FUNGAL INTRUDERS

Dear Readers,

Molds, mildews, yeasties—it seems that this spring, all is wet and warm, and the pH is rising in your private places. This may be a cause of concern for you, but I say sometimes the spore's the merrier.

Q. Dear Mertensia, there were some brain-looking toadstools that came up in my yard. I was going to spray them, but then they just disappeared overnight. What are they, and is this going to be a recurring problem? —*Cromwell, Hamford*

A. Dear "Cromwell," there was no missing what happened here, since an entire day was ruined by the roar of a chainsaw massacre next door. You had the only remaining mature elm tree in the city cut down as a "preventative measure" against Dutch elm disease. This is a bit like having your leg amputated as a preventative against toenail fungus. The toadstools you are worried about were morel mushrooms which grew over the rotting elm roots, and, knowing you wouldn't appreciate them, they disappeared into a little butter and cream on toast points. I fervently wish the morels would be a recurring problem, but I'm sure you will be hiring a crew to come in, grind the stump down, and dig up the remaining roots.

❧❧❧

Q: After the heavy rain last week, a large circle of mushrooms appeared in my lawn (snapshot enclosed). I kicked it all over and then stomped it flat, but then I wonder whether I should spray the area with a fungicide to prevent it from coming back. —*Chuck, Glengarry*

A: The toadstool colony which you marched over like a horticultural Wehrmacht is called a fairy ring. Judging from the photo you sent, it was definitely the most interesting thing that ever occurred in that patch of Astroturf you call a lawn. You might have pried your children away from the TV set long enough to see the fairy ring, enchanting them with impromptu stories of pixies coming to visit. But I suppose their imaginations have been jack-booted by you as well. This is absolutely the last lawn-care question I will entertain, and that's final.

❧❧❧

Q: I will be vacationing in the English Cotswolds this summer, and I would like to bring back some hard-to-find plant specimens. I understand this is a touchy issue with customs. Couldn't I just airmail a package to myself, declaring it to be something else?

I know that's not exactly legal, but what's the harm if the plants come from a nursery that stays on top of diseases and insect pests?
—*Maurice, Connersville*

A. Dear Maurice, rules are rules. Check with the nursery in question to see if they have the licensing to ship live plants to you, properly packaged and labeled. You might get away with your little scheme, but there also might be some keen-nosed German shepherd at the airport who is working on his third merit biscuit and a big promotion. Sometimes these things can backfire on you. When I was a boarding school student, several of my schoolmates and I accompanied our botany teacher, Sister Marie Tanguay, on a summer field trip to Japan. Sister Marie found an interesting specimen of stinkhorn (*Phallus impudicus*) to add to the convent herbarium collection of non-lichen fungi.

In a bit of deception, Sister Marie shipped the specimen in its surrounding forest soil to herself, falsely labeling the contents on the customs form as folk art. The package languished at the post office for months, the address partially obscured by humidity. There was an attempted delivery to an all-male styling salon and spa, Tan Guy. The rest of the address was garbled: Sisters of Concern…Merry Mount…Hamford… USA. The stinkhorn had begun to live up to its name, the salon refused delivery, and the package was returned to the Hamford Post Office. As time passed, the stinkhorn grew, erupting in its full-blown glory from the packaging to the astonishment of the parcel-sorting staff, leading to an outbreak of violence. Eventually the *Phallus impudicus* was delivered to the school, causing Mother Superior to swoon, requiring emergency resuscitation and extra novenas, not to mention the severe penance imposed on Sister Marie. I hope you will reconsider any ideas about illegally importing plant material.

GLEANINGS:

Still wondering what exactly is a fairy ring? Beneath the fruit of the fungus, the mushrooms that you can see above ground, lies a huge mass called a mycelium.

Chemicals released by the mycelium feed the mushrooms and break down other plant life in its path. There is a ring in France that is nearly a half mile in diameter and estimated to be as much as seven hundred years old. I think it's entirely possible that medieval fairies plopped down on the toadstools to rest during a night of merry dancing in a ring.

Next time ... Wellington boots vs. French sabots, the footwear controversy ... garden monument ideas for your pet's cremains

RADICAL PRUNINGS

APRIL 5

Gardening Advice by Mertensia Corydalis

TULIPS IN BONDAGE

Dear Readers,

There seems to be a revival of tulipomania, not quite as financially ruinous as that which gripped Holland in the seventeenth century, although I always seem to buy a hundred more bulbs than planned each fall. We are inundated with questions about tulips this spring. I wish more of you would plant species tulips such as *Tulipa turkestanica, T. tarda,* and *T. bakeri.* Long-lived, they are hardy, early blooming, and are of more subtle coloration than their commercially hybridized cousins. True, they are smaller, but you don't need blooms big enough to be photographed from a speeding tour bus. By this time of year, you should be more than ready to take a stroll, stop, admire. On to some of your questions now, and at the end, some suggestions from your Miss Mertensia.

Q: Dear Mertensia, last fall I planted rows of tulip bulbs in front of my house and lining the driveway. Now they are coming up this spring in random clumps in the beds. I'm just fit to be tied. I'll bet squirrels are the culprits. Can I do something to prevent this from happening again? —*Brenda, Pennington*

A: Brenda, years ago I never imagined that, in my lifetime, in the same sentence, I would ever hear the words "President" and "penis." But even more jarring is the juxtaposition of the words "tulip" and "row." Your neighbors, the squirrels, have the advantage over you in landscaping your property. They are outdoors all the time; they get both extreme close-up looks at your flower beds as well as large overviews from the vantage point of trees. Thus, they are in a much better position than you to make aesthetic decisions about gardening. Plus, unlike you, the squirrels instinctively know that unstudied groupings of odd numbers of bulbs are far more pleasing to the eye than lines of goose-stepping Red Emperor tulips parading past the reviewing stand.

≈≈≈≈

Q: When our spring bulbs have finished blooming, what's the best way to deal with the foliage as it dies back? I say it looks neater to gather the leaves together and fasten them with a rubber band. My wife says I'm a retentive and that it's better for the plant to just let them turn into an ugly, unruly, yellowing, rotting spectacle. —*Rafe and Silvana, vallone@neorealism.net*

A: Well, your wife does have a point. While the dying foliage is not the most attractive thing, it serves a purpose to leave it alone. Photosynthesis, my friend. Spring bulb flowers have a lot of leaf surface, which is needed to feed the bulb for next year's bloom. Turning them into little packages like banana-leaf dumplings is not exactly a natural look either and certainly deprives the plant of nutrition. Next fall, plant your bulbs among perennials which will cover up the dying leaves as their own foliage emerges.

Now is the time to plan your autumn bulb-buying spree. Take pictures or make sketches of what you have now. Did someone reach into the bargain bin of mixed tulips and now you have a bed that looks like a bad bowl of jellybeans, all your least-favorite flavors? Be bold and yank out the ones you don't like. Instead, how about a clutch of white, cream, and green-tinged viridifloras?

Or how about a massive bouquet of strawberry, raspberry, and rose colors? If you only have ten dollars to spend, fill up a paper bag with ten dollars' worth of Chinese red lily-flowered tulips and make a splash, planting them all in one spot. It's your canvas to paint as you please.

Dear Readers,

I wish to share this distressing event in order that you may contemplate and learn. A few days ago, as I glanced out my kitchen window, I saw a large cloud of mist in my neighbor's yard. When the mist blew to one side, there was the whitest white man I have ever seen, dressed in a kelly green jumpsuit, drenching a large arborvitae with spray. He had no breathing mask, no respirator, and not one hair on his head. I called my dogs indoors immediately, in a panic over the spreading poisonous cloud. And we were ready to go to war over chemical and biological weapons five thousand miles away! Well, Mr. Greenjeans will pay for his evil job, carcinogens going first for the gonads.

But what about the multitude of birds who dwell within the arborvitae? Where would those who were not immediately suffocated seek shelter against the night's cold and wind? And there are already egg and sperm on the runway for this year's crop of baby birds!

GLEANINGS:

The fantastic feathering and flames on the petals of tulips you have seen in old Dutch still-life paintings is known as "breaking." Broken tulips, or Bizarres, were the most highly prized.

Little did their fanciers know that the colorful variegations were caused by a viral disease.

In my own garden, I find the modern hybridized imitators of broken tulips are short-lived and often stillborn, victims of tulip fire, the fungal *botrytis* blight. When your heart is broken by the diseased tulips, there is nothing to do but remove them from the garden entirely and wait at least two years before replanting tulips in that area. The spores will die, and you'll get over it.

Next time ... reflections on nematodes ... mucking out your pond

RADICAL PRUNINGS

APRIL 11

Gardening Advice by Mertensia Corydalis

THE GREAT VIOLET INVASION

Dear Readers,

This is going to be one of the finest garden years ever. Lingering deep snow insulated our perennials from the most extreme cold, and while the abundant rain may encourage diseases like black spot and powdery mildew, proper management can reduce even these problems.

Tran is arriving not long after daybreak and working until sunset, barely stopping for lunch.

We are hosting Open Day this year as a fundraiser for the Hamford Center for Disruptive Children. Miss Vong will be placing announcements with the details in this newsletter and the *Hamford Cornet.* This is a rare opportunity for you to visit my garden, enjoy a cup of punch, and purchase a signed copy of one of my books, as well as to provide harmless diversions for annoyingly disruptive children.

Q: Dear Mertensia, I found a charming iron terrace table and chair set which someone had tossed in the rubbish. It has a considerable amount of rust and chipped paint. I see in the home design magazines that this au naturel look is in vogue. What do you think? —*J.A. Prufrock, Brighton*

A: Alfred, what nonsense these interior decorators perpetrate upon the public! If you leave the set as is, and should you wear white flannel trousers, they will be ruined by rust stains. Sand the furniture down and paint it. Giverny blue-green would be a nice color choice. Do not be so slavish to the opinions of others. Take a walk on the beach. Eat a peach. You're not getting any younger.

❧❧❧

Q: I have a Bing cherry tree that looks like it's going to be loaded with fruit this year. How can I keep the birds away? The tree is too large to cover with netting. I have seen inflatable owls and snakes in the nursery stores. Do they work?
—*Dave, Mt. Victory*

A: Dave, here is how it works: the top third of the tree is for the birds; the bottom third is for your dogs and visiting raccoons. The middle third of the tree is yours, which conveniently you can reach without a ladder. Don't be greedy. At the end of the one week when the cherries will be ripe, you and everyone you know will be sick of eating them. And if the wildlife hadn't pollinated the cherry blossoms, you wouldn't

TRAP NIGHT
CRAWLERS UNDER
FLOWER POT.

have any fruit at all. Save your money for an inflatable girlfriend. It would offer you greater utility than the items you mentioned in your query.

❧❧❧

Q. Miss Corydalis, you know how invasive wild violets can be. My lawn, which I had rolled and completely reseeded last year, is a sea of little purple flowers this spring. What can I use to kill them? —*Wallace, Upper Lexington*

A. Wallace, I believe you misdirected your question. You want to contact the wall-to-wall carpeting column. This is a gardening column. Here, we welcome a good ravaging by little purple flowers. Did Colette confide to her journals fond memories of Kentucky bluegrass nosegays? Did Proust bury his Gallic nose in a bunch of rye-grass blend? Enough of these tiresome lawn-care questions. No more!

COOKERY

The wild violets you encounter on your walks in the spring are not protected, at least as far as I'm concerned, and I won't report you if you pluck a few to transform into candied violets and elevate your humble cupcakes into something worthy of the appellation "pastry." Simply gently rinse and let dry on paper towels violets you pick growing wild. (Do not use violets that have grown in lawns or flower beds that have been sprayed with pesticides or treated with other chemicals!) Whisk an egg white with a teaspoon of water until it is barely frothy. With a small artist's brush, coat each violet completely with the egg white, then sprinkle with superfine white sugar to coat. Dry the flowers on a rack for at least a day (a humid atmosphere may require a long drying time). Store the violets in an airtight tin for up to a year. You will find yourself wishing you had even more violets in your lawn.

This is a fun project for your children, but they must be old enough to understand that one does not indiscriminately eat flowers from the garden.

Next time ... antiquing for vintage flamingos ... growing the right cucumber for your needs

RADICAL PRUNINGS

APRIL 20

Gardening Advice by Mertensia Corydalis

BLESSED EVENTS

Dear Readers,

The soil is not quite warm enough to plant corn, but it's not too early to make your plans and buy seed.

My French grandfather (Maman's father) made his only visit to America one summer when I was a child. I remember him scolding Maman for allowing Artie and me to gnaw on ears of corn like barnyard animals. True, this was a practice unknown to our British father and French mother, but immigrants eventually succumb to the demands of their children for American food that they eat at school and at their friends' homes. I recall being dazzled, briefly, by the idea of melted Velveeta sandwiches.

Anyway, when I am in the mood for a little clandestine gnawing, I pull back the corn husks enough to expose the kernels and remove as much of the silk as possible and rinse the ear, leaving it damp. (Artie and I briefly experimented with smoking the brown silks in the seclusion of the mostly ignored

Japanese teahouse Father had built one summer, but this practice is not recommended.) Season the kernels with salt, pepper, melted butter, and any other embellishment you may desire. One of my Chinese friends says her family swipes hoisin on the kernels before grilling the ears. After seasoning the corn, pull the husks back over the ear, twist the ends, and grill on the barbecue or roast in a hot oven for about ten minutes.

Q: Dear Mertensia, we love to cook stir-fry style. Can we grow our own baby corn? Is there a special variety of corn to plant? —*Vivian & Bettina, North Campus*

A: Any variety of sweet corn seed will do. Plant the seeds closely, say eight inches on center. Pick within a few days after the ears have begun to silk and are about three inches long. Remember to rotate your crops and plant a legume in the same spot next year. Edamame (edible soybeans) would be an excellent choice.

This brings me to something that makes me a little peckish: supermarket shoppers pawing over sweet corn, stripping back the husks as if they had any idea what they might find that would make the ear unacceptable to someone who has never been closer to a farm than two freeway interchanges. By the way, aren't you two the ladies who installed my cable TV?

❧❧❧

Q: My rather flamboyant little wife has brought home several wildly expensive blooming orchid plants (which we could ill afford, I might add). Is there any chance that they can be made to rebloom later? The plants are in our solarium, which has a textbook microclimate. —*T.C., Birwyck*

A. T.C., it is easier to produce a human baby than it is to get a potted orchid to rebloom (although if you are of an advanced age, the odds might favor the orchid). But have hope. Miss Corydalis had two blessed events so far this year, thanks to loving orchid husbandry by Tran (after years of buying plants at considerable prices, and my own rather neglectful care, I must confess). If you do get a bloom, place the pot where you can look into the flower at eye level, that you might revel in its intricacies. Orchid flowers imitate some other things, such as the larger, more attractive insects, with bristling wings, sturdy little legs as thin as copper filaments, pudenda, etc. I once read that some orchids are so desperate to be pollinated they will literally throw themselves at a passing insect. Ladies, haven't we all?

❧❧❧

Q. Enclosed is a bug I caught chewing my roses. I showed it to the lawn-care guy and he said we need to get on a more frequent program of spraying for grubs. He said grubs are the larvae of this bug. What do you think? —*Mike, Eastgrove*

A. This is not technically a lawn question, so I will include your letter in this issue. The beautiful blue and green iridescent carapace (crushed by the mail-canceling machinery) you enclosed belongs to a Japanese beetle. Such insects can indeed cause considerable damage to your roses. The best way to deal with the problem is to purchase a Japanese beetle trap at the nursery. While your neighbor is away at work, choose a discreet location in his yard and install the trap. This will lure the vandals away from your roses. You know how Miss C. feels about spraying programs.

I am to reminding you, your letter can get lost at our office if you ask about grass any more.

—Miss Francine Vong,
Special Assistance to
Miss Mertensia

Next time ... growing window box potatoes ... deadly gas buildup in your pond

RADICAL PRUNINGS

APRIL 26

Gardening Advice by Mertensia Corydalis

ANTS IN YOUR PLANTS

Dear Readers,

This time we will proceed directly to your questions, as we have an exciting announcement at the end of this newsletter. Let's begin with a phenomenon that many new gardeners find puzzling.

Q. Dear Mertensia, I just moved into my first own home. In the yard is a bed of what a neighbor tells me are peonies. They have big ball-shaped buds that have ants on them. I don't see ants on the other plants. Should I be concerned?
—*Roberta, North Lynden*

A. First, Roberta, resist the temptation to rip out everything the previous owner left in the way of plant material. Let a year pass and study what you have. It is possible that the peony bed has been in place for generations, in which case you have a bit of a moral obligation to be the caretaker of plants set out with loving high hopes by a long-forgotten housewife. As for the ants, they enjoy a symbiosis with the peonies, tickling and teasing the tightly contained buds until they open themselves in a wanton, blowsy shag of petals, seducing the gardener to plunge his nose in their midst and swoon, nearly overcome by the headiness of their scent. The payoff for the ants? They can busy themselves collecting the sweet juices of the peony, toiling in working conditions that rival a seraglio.

༺༒༒༒༺

Q. Which is better: caging or staking tomato plants? I plan to grow giant beefsteak tomatoes. I would like to see just how big I can get them to grow. Would the fruit need special support?
—*Walter, Willow Grove*

A. Just what kind of Brobdingnagian club sandwiches do you plan to prepare with these freaks of botanical tinkering? I should be surprised if this "bigger is better" philosophy of yours doesn't carry over to other aspects of your life. Being a backyard gardener, you have the advantage of not having to deliver the tomatoes three thousand miles by freight car to your table, so you also don't need to grow the tasteless baseballs known as Big Boy, Better Boy, Boy Toy, and all the other engineered "Boy" members of the deadly-nightshade family. Look into heirloom varieties such as Costoluto Genovese, Brandywine, Yellow Pear, and enjoy them still warm from the sun.

DUST GUN

COOKERY

Real tomato fanatics take a salt shaker into the garden and eat the fruit at its juciest. If you can exercise a little patience, reward yourself with this presentation.

There is nothing more simple or more pleasing to the eye and the palate than a variety of tomatoes, such as the ones named above and others like Green Zebra, Crimean Black, and Orange Oxheart, sliced and beautifully arranged, alternating with slices of fresh buffalo mozzarella cheese, sprinkled with salt and pepper, a chiffonade of fresh basil, and drizzled with olive oil.

Grow something new this year.

And now to our announcement:

When I maligned the orange-colored Tropicana rose, I

had no idea how many of you would rush to its defense. After my initial bewilderment, I decided that what you need is to get it out of your systems, so I am announcing a contest. Those orange-color flower fans among you, design and plant out a monochrome bed, a "Lucille Ball Memorial Garden." Some rose suggestions, besides the Tropicana: Cary Grant and Caribe (another nod to Desi). A few other plant ideas: the orange poppy, *Asclepias* (the butterfly weed), lilies (both Asiatic and *hemerocallis*). Send me snapshots and a plant list before the first killing frost. To the best I will award a nice trowel from the Mertensia Post Haste signature line of garden accessories.

So there you have your mission. Astonish me. Amuse me. Convince me.

Next time ...creating a mossy dell ...winning the black-spot war

RADICAL PRUNINGS

MAY 3

Gardening Advice by Mertensia Corydalis

TURF CREATURES

Dear Readers,

Our rock-and-roll star's garden makeover project is moving forward. The first major hurdle was restaffing the groundskeeping crew, mostly with Tran's soccer mates. It was not a cordial transition. You cannot imagine how difficult it is to find a replacement set of whitewall tires to fit my Buick Roadmaster. The lagoon has been drained and dredged of plant debris and undergarments, and a bevy of swans is on order. A sculpture of Leda in a saucy pose, previously in the fountain of an Italian fashion designer gone bankrupt, was sent over on approval by a London auction house. There immediately formed a pro-Leda faction: the property owner a.k.a. the Big Cheese and his cymbal-polishing sycophants, the new groundskeepers, and, in a momentary lapse of taste, not to mention loyalty, my very own Tran, all voting to keep the sculpture. But they were up against the anti-Leda faction: Me. There were long faces when the statue was crated up and trucked away, but this garden is my creation and I have the last word.

On to our letters:

Q: Dear Mertensia, we are brand new to these parts and have inherited an apple orchard on our property. Last summer, our first here, the apples only got to about one and a half inches in diameter, then fell off the tree before ripening. Also, I've noticed several snakes in the orchard, which makes me nervous. We're having a little dispute over this. I say we cut down the orchard. My wife is just dying to have her own apples. What's your opinion? —*Adam, St. Paris*

A: It sounds like your apple blossoms are not getting properly pollinated. You can rent a hive from a beekeeper, who will install and maintain it during the blossoming period. See if this doesn't solve the problem before taking to the ax. The snakes are no doubt harmless and serve the useful purpose of keeping down the population of field mice which feast on the fallen, rotting apples.

Regardless of my opinion, I suspect that your wife usually wins out in these domestic disputes anyway.

❧❧❧❧

Q: While working on my lawn this morning, I unearthed a whole gaggle of white larvae. I got out my old *Big Book of Bugs* which I've had since childhood and identified the larvae as Australian witchiti grubs. (Did you know that the natives there eat them!) Am I going to have to have the whole lawn fumigated and new sod laid? —*Kingsley, Hamford*

A: "Kingsley," just how are these Australian witty-titty grubs supposed to have turned up on your lawn? I think what you have there are the grubs of Japanese beetles, and I'm not very happy about that, because in no time flat the beetles will be over here eating my roses. Go get some milky spore at the garden center. This is a bacterium which will do in the grubs eventually. It is hardly necessary to lay all new sod, but no advice I might give you would be heeded anyway. By the way, it's about time you add a grown-up book on insects to your garden library, particularly one which narrows the topic down to, say, North America. And your *Masterpiece Theatre* pseudonyms do not fool me for a moment. I'm making an exception this one time, but if I see one more lawn-care question in my mailbag, I shall toss it out unread.

GLEANINGS:

Did you know…the apple, the rose, and the strawberry are all in the same family?

If you don't believe me, compare the blossom end of the nascent apple, the hip of the rose, and the calyx of the strawberry.

Next time… creating a pleached allée… Sussex trugs

RADICAL PRUNINGS

MAY 9

Gardening Advice by Mertensia Corydalis

A LITTLE AERATION CAN'T HURT

Some months ago, Miss Vong taped a magazine photo, mounted on cardboard, to her computer monitor. The picture is a close-up of a woman's beautifully manicured hand, the thumb and forefinger forming the OK sign. It is a common practice in Vietnam to display a paper image of the object of your dreams. When she first came to work as my secretary, she displayed a magazine photo of a handsome actor, shirtless, cut out and mounted onto cardboard like the paper dolls I played with as a child. It was an unqualified success, as the real boy dolls materialized and melted away in dizzying succession.

On Miss Vong's desk are snapshots of her life and family in Vietnam. There is a picture of Francine, as a teenager, seated beneath a paddle fan in her mother's rustic office, typing invoices for flowers on her pre World War II Olivetti. She is surrounded by galvanized buckets of flowers and one can almost feel and smell the heat and closeness of the fragrances.

In another photo, she and all her brothers (the last child, Miss Vong is the only girl) and Madame Bich stand in front of a field of vivid blooms. The farm has survived the Chinese, the Japanese, the French, a runaway husband, the Americans, gold-digging lovers, and the Communists. There's a flower seller on every corner in Saigon, she tells me, and whatever else happens, there will always be weddings and funerals and romances. Tran is easy to pick out—he's the most handsome one, with the long hair pulled back. She tells me one is supposed to get a haircut for New Year's, Tet, but Tran was too proud of his hair to allow more than a tiny bit to be cut off each year. She didn't know the English word for "vanity."

Tran's early experiments in pollination got to be too much of a distraction for the country girls who cut and bundled the flowers, so Madame Bich made a huge financial sacrifice and sent him to the city to study horticulture. Miss Vong talked her way into going to the city, too.

She liked to ride on the back of motorbikes, clinging to the waists of the kind of boys who rode café racers, who smoked American cigarettes and called up girls on their cell phones. No, she was not the sort of girl to be content in a dingy office, typing up invoices for ginger lilies.

Now, for the curious, an update on our Rock Garden project:

As with interior designers, it is important for the garden designer to solicit input from the client. Long after the final check has been rushed to the bank, the client is the one who has to live with the project. The results should reflect the client's personality and station in life. But sometimes one must put one's foot down.

We have had to exercise our veto power on the idea of speakers concealed in artificial boulders all over the landscape. Miss Mertensia does not permit any sounds in the garden louder than infant robins demanding their breakfast, the splash of a fountain, or the rustle of dried grasses. We had to send some bush whacking artist packing—he showed up uninvited with a truckload of potted Kama Sutra topiaries. (Although there was one, if viewed from a certain angle…well, anyway, they're gone.)

Let us return to projects on a more human scale: the home garden.

Q. Dear Mertensia, how do you get a pond ready for spring?
—*Felicia, Clayton*

A. Inspect the pump and filtration system, replacing any cracked tubing and cleaning out any debris. Next you must remove the autumn leaves that have blown in. If the pond is small, lift out the leaves with a rake or even a doggie pooper scooper. Here, my garden assistant Tran and I first remove the pots of *Iris kaempferi* and water lilies so they will not be disturbed by the thrashing about. Then, because my pond is virtually bottomless, Tran strips to the waist and, wearing no waders, plunges right in and goes at it, taking care not to puncture the butyl liner. There will be a bit of musky odor, but consider it part of getting the job done. Add the leaves and muck to your compost heap or apply them directly to the base of your plants, the rich, decomposing material like truffles fed to a lover; the rewards will be generous.

Q. Miss Corydalis, a friend tells me I need to have my lawn aerated. The lawn-care companies want to charge several hundred dollars for this. I saw these aerating do-it-yourself devices you can mail order. [The reader enclosed the catalogue illustration.] Do you think they will work? —*Buck, Greater Maumee*

A. Buck, since your lawn is out-of-doors most of the time, it's getting plenty of air. I suppose we're talking about thatch build up, which would not be a problem if you were not having the turf bombarded with nitrogen four times a year. The illustration—from the sort of catalogue that sells ice cube molds in the form of breasts and Denver Broncos toiletbrush concealers—is of a pair of spiked platforms which one buckles onto the soles of one's shoes. If you don't mind spending the afternoon doing a frenzied flamenco dance in full view of all your neighbors, you might manage to loosen up the thatch a bit. Otherwise, fire the chemical warfare service and let Nature take its course. Finally, you have a lot of cheek sending me another damned lawn-care question.

Next time ... a knot garden how-to ... espalier your medlar

RADICAL PRUNINGS

MAY 17

Gardening Advice by Mertensia Corydalis

YARD-LONG BEANS

Dear Readers,

Many of you have written to inquire about the publication date of my forthcoming book on *Pulmonaria*. Check your local newspaper garden pages for my illustrated lecture tour and book-signing schedule, as well as this newsletter. The book has been delayed because every time I turn my back on the lungworts they crossbreed, resulting in still more varieties to classify.

In addition, there have been distractions. There is a tiresome tax agent questioning my new plant purchases being written off as research and development and insisting that my gardener's wages be classified as an entertainment expense. I will let my accountant, Ms. Marvell, take care of that matter.

Then there are the collect calls from Bangkok by my brother Artur, begging me to wire money for some special antibiotic ointment and to bring his hotel bill up to date. It will do Artie good to just wait a bit and let his anxiety level rise. Maybe this time he'll learn his lesson and not go overboard on room service.

Q. Dear Mertensia, we're crazy about our new wok—a housewarming gift—and are perfecting our Chinese cooking skills. Can we grow yard-long beans in our garden? —*Margot and Bettina, North Campus*

A. What a thoughtful gift! Yes, yard-long beans (actually only about eighteen inches long), or asparagus beans as they are also known, are cultivated in the same way as our more familiar green beans. You must train the plants to a support at least thirty inches tall, so that the beans will be suspended as they develop. You don't need anything elaborate. Small branches, twigs and all, the prunings from trees and bushes can be poked into the ground. Weave some string in the brush. The bean plants will figure out the rest of it. I see from your letterhead that Margot is a glazier. I must talk with you about my cold frame.

Dear Readers,

One of the least attractive aspects of American culture is the seizing of any opportunity, every moment of the day, to sell something. There is no escaping it. I recently had occasion to attend a luncheon for horticulture journalists held at the estate of Mrs. Delphine Doyle, the publisher doyenne of *Gracious Way Magazine*. The purpose of the luncheon was to show off the newly refurbished gardens designed by GW garden editor, Norton Doyle, husband of Delphine (and my former husband). Well, Mrs. Doyle, née Ruby Schmidt, always willing to accept a subsidy in exchange for advertising, has allowed little signs to be placed all over the gardens, e.g., on boxwood obelisks (certainly a fiction of Norton's): PRUNED WITH A FELCO. Amidst the aconitum: FERTILIZED WITH VIGORO. The beds EDGED BY TORO, and so on. I found it appalling (and the gardens were stiff and pretentious, not unlike their designer). But in an effort to be generous, I will nominate Mrs. Doyle for the Silver Hoe award. Miss Vong continues to put your lawn-care questions in a separate, and unread, pile.

Next time ... an exultation of larkspur... foiling cutworms

RADICAL PRUNINGS

MAY 25

Gardening Advice by Mertensia Corydalis

EAST MEETS WEST

On to your growing concerns:

Q: **Dear Mertensia, stir-fried spinach is a favorite here and we grow our own. The problem is that when the weather gets really hot, the spinach goes right to seed. Is there anything we can do?** —*Margot and Lana, North Campus*

A: I see that Bettina is no longer with us. You can try shading your spinach in the hottest months by using a fabric row-cover setup, which can be purchased at a nursery. You can also improvise a shade with old sheeting stretched on a frame, propped at an angle. Sowing the seed in the shade cast by taller plants, such as trellised peas or tomatoes, might improve the yield. Best would be to grow a substitute such as Japanese entsai or komatsuna. By the way, isn't Lana the carpenter who installed my pet door?

❧❧❧

Q: **Please suggest some varieties of cucumber which are not seedy and bitter.** —*Marianne, Galloway*

A: A common variety is the lemon cucumber. If picked fairly small, it might answer your requirements. Tran, my garden assistant, introduced me to the Asian cucumber, which is a slim fruit. It is crisp and mild-tasting and, unlike the English hothouse variety, which I used to prefer, it does not wilt readily.

❧❧❧

Which brings me to some news. I noticed the sylphid Miss Vong was getting plump about the middle. Yesterday she made us a little tea, with a snack of julienned cucumber dressed with a bit of *nuoc mam*, the Vietnamese fish sauce, wrapped in moistened rice papers. It seems that young Mr. Troung, hoping to qualify for residency status, seduced Miss Vong. Mr. Troung is in detention, and Miss Vong, suffice to say, is distraught. Her brother Tran is set on slitting Mr. Troung stem to stern with a grafting knife, gutting him like a Tet festival suckling pig. The fate of all three seems to be in the tiny fist of Miss Vong's "surprise." In a future column I will write about the cornichon.

This column has turned out to have an Oriental theme. So, since no one in the Far East has an interest in vast expanses of lawn (except for a few plastic toy manufacturers in Singapore), we will pass on the lawn-care questions.

Next time ... nettles and docks ... double digging

RADICAL PRUNINGS

MAY 30

Gardening Advice by Mertensia Corydalis

THE MOONFLOWER

Dear Readers,

We have made so many visits to our design project this spring that the gates to the estate swing wide open the moment the red nose of my Buick Roadmaster appears at the bend down the road. Miss Vong, always along in case I need notes taken in Vietnamese shorthand, breezily announces to the guard: "We're with the band."

The hardscaping (pathways, rock-wall repairs, etc.) is complete and the trees have either been rejuvenated or replaced. We have created little secluded areas of dense shrubbery and brightly colored benches for trysting. New plumbing in the center of the lagoon shoots a series of celebratory jets into the air.

A happy surprise resulted from searching for Miss Vong on one of our trips to the estate. She was supposed to be taking notes, but seems to have disappeared into the carriage house with Herr Rubric, the chef. In the carriage house we found a cache of whimsical sculptures made of scrap metal and wood, all brightly painted with hardware store enamels, constructed by an ardent fan of El Queso Grande. There are enough rootin' tootin' bare-chested cowgirl angels to anchor each perennial bed, and an Adam and Eve, dressed only in pearls and briefcase, being expelled from Eden in a huff. We'll put this at the entrance to the garden.

And just when I was beginning to question the wisdom of bringing along Miss Vong!

For the herbaceous beds, we offered our client, a.k.a. the Big Cheese, a palette of colors from which he was permitted to select his favorites. He chose the purples and chartreuse of a spectacular bruise he suffered after falling off a stage in Hamburg, even giving us copies of the tabloid photos for reference. The client was extremely pleased with Tran's watercolor sketches of succession planting, giving a constant display of color throughout the growing season. There will be blotches of the deepest purple aconitum and delphinium in the center of each bed, blending into eruptions of magenta malva, scabiosa and swellings of violet phlox, with stains of lady's mantle and variegated yellow and green striped carex at the edges. Miss Gertrude Jekyll must be spinning in her grave, but then she never designed a garden for Le Grand Fromage.

Your letters:

Q. Dear Mertensia, I'd appreciate advice to a beginning composter. —*Danielle, Italian Village*

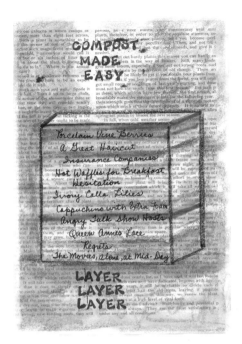

A. Welcome to our fold, Danielle! Good compost is like rocket fuel when applied to your plants. There is never enough of it, and you will find yourself rationing it out, giving a little extra to your favorites. Don't bother with tedious recipes for layering brown and green vegetation. You are not making a *pousse café*. Just toss in leaves, garden tidyings, and the salad ingredients you bought to start your new diet, now decomposing in the fridge as you revert to your usual fare of frozen lasagna. Bin or rough pile, no matter, time is on your side. Dig out from the bottom, throwing back big chunks. Eventually everything organic will compost, as will you. As will I.

Q. This past spring, my husband planted moonflower seeds. Summer is slipping through my fingers. Evenings I lie under the stars, the earth my comforter, and watch the luminescent flowers slowly unfurl themselves, only to be spent by sunrise. [Note: the reader then launched into a lengthy, bitter account of the husband leaving her for another man, which Miss C. has edited out.] Will the moonflowers return next spring?

—*Patricia, New Portugal*

A. My poor Patricia. I suspect you are an artist or literary type, as no one else fancies his childhood so wretched, his affairs of the heart so tragic, his sex life so varied, or his constipation so intractable that others will not only desire that he share these experiences, but will gladly pay admission to the sharing, as well. Get up, take a bath, and get into a proper bed, preferably with a new love. Moonflowers are annuals. They will not return next spring.

❧❧❧

Q. There is a strip between my house and the neighbor's which is nearly covered with thick moss. I would like to sow grass seed there so I could make that area part of my weekly mowing. What's the best product to use to keep the moss from coming back?

—*Steve, Grandview*

A. Why anyone would want to expand the dreadful task of lawn mowing is beyond me. Apparently, Nature has found a most hospitable location to give you the gift of a soft, velvety green path. And a nearly maintenance-free path,

I might add. Just a gentle raking to remove any autumn leaves is all that is required. Make a special trip to the library and find a picture of the Saiho-ji Moss Temple garden in Kyoto. You will thank Providence that a thousand years ago no one shopped for a product to get that moss under control and fired up the Lawnboy.

Miss Mertensia say this is Moss Question,
not Lawn Question, so OK to answer.

—*Miss Francine Vong*

GLEANINGS:

Cat Barometer: In fifteenth-century France, it was believed that if your cat scratched behind her ear, you could count on rain. A nervous cat signaled heavy winds approaching. And if you saw your cat scratching the dirt amidst your leeks and carrots, a storm was imminent. Or something else.

Next time ... sundials, armillaries, and astrolabes ...
cardoons

RADICAL PRUNINGS

JUNE 2

Gardening Advice by Mertensia Corydalis

THE LAST TANGO IN BUENOS AIRES

Q: Dear Mertensia, finding myself with a lot of time on my hands, I'd like to take up indoor gardening as a hobby—specifically, growing medicinal herbs. My window only gets a few hours of sun a day and my resources are very limited. Any ideas?
—*John, #895477, Lucasville*

A: John, very few people know this, but during the Falkland Islands fracas, I was a botanical rescue volunteer. Upon my arrival via commercial flight to Buenos Aires, the authorities prevented my boarding a commuter hop to the Falklands. I was detained a short time in an Argentine police station. (The guards were entirely civil, and I even had a good turn at tango with a guard named Rogelio.) To pass the time I started pots of gazania daisies in my window. I made do with a light reflector fashioned from the cardboard backing of notepads and bits of aluminum foil from Cadbury chocolate wrappers, using gravy as the adhesive. I hope this is helpful.

Q: This is the third year for my lilac bush. Last year it bloomed, but this year, nothing. I mulched and fertilized it, and last fall I shaped it up with pruners. —*Nigel, Hamford*

A: Well, now you've done it, "Nigel"! The buds for next year's bloom begin to form immediately after this year's flush of flowers. The little styling you gave the bush last fall whacked off this year's buds. Also, save your energy. The mulching and fertilizing are unnecessary, although a few handfuls of lime would be appreciated.

Speaking of whacking, you have amputated my Nelly Moser clematis *twice* by insinuating your nylon string trimmer under my fence. If there is a repeat, I shall have to resort to retaliatory measures.

Readers: while visiting a public garden. I was inspired by a service area which was paved with turf blocks. These are flat concrete blocks with hollow square centers in which grass is planted. They allow groundsmen's vehicles to pass without making muddy tracks. When mowed flush, a checked design is created. When the grass is allowed to grow a bit longer, the blocks are nearly concealed. Imagine if the freeways within the city were built this way, how much more civil motorists would be, driving to work on a swath of green. Perhaps this would put an end to ugly incidents involving lady accountants juggling cell phones and applying their mascara while receiving faxes on the front seat, gunning down anyone who cuts in front of them on the highway.

Next time...using convolvulus and nemophilia to attract hoverflies

RADICAL PRUNINGS

JUNE 6

Gardening Advice by Mertensia Corydalis

THE HOLE'S THE THING

Dear Readers,

Bibi Mazoon is dead.

Dead.

The same fate befell Sharifa Asma. No progeny of David Austin should meet such premature demise. Oh, my money was cheerfully refunded, but the sting of dashed anticipation is still there. I am loath to order bare-root roses again from a certain mail-order nursery, the one with the best free color catalogue and the mouth-watering selection of English and antique roses.

This brings me to the mailbag full of questions about roses. The current controversy seems to be regarding the hole in which you plant your new rose. First, bare-root or potted? Well, bare-root is all right, so long as the plant is still dormant. But you are instructed to build a cone of soil in the bottom of the hole, over which you arrange the roots. Have you ever tried to create this fiction of us garden writers, bent over, resting on your bony knees? And the graft. Below the soil level or above?

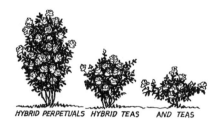

HYBRID PERPETUALS   HYBRID TEAS   AND TEAS

3 TYPES OF BEDDING ROSES

Have you left deadly pockets of air? Go with the pot-grown rose. Strip down the pressed paper pot and toss it on your compost pile.

Now, the next controversy: Tough Love or Indulgence. The Tough Love School contends that if you dig an appropriately sized hole, line it with compost, plant the rose, backfill with your beautifully amended topsoil, fertilize, and mulch, the adolescent rose will be so content with these cushy conditions, it will never send its roots beyond this hole to investigate new sources of nutrition, soon to be dead from a dissipated youth. The Indulgent School maintains that if you provide the rose with your best homemade black gold compost, your loveliest humus-rich backfill, it will grow on to expect the best that life can provide and smile back on the world with great flourishes of blooms for years to come. You decide.

Q: We have planted a redwood tree in our growing collection of specimens. Do you have any cultural advice?
—*Bunny, Birwyck*

A: Dear Bunny, with this question you have caught Miss Corydalis with her knickers down. I've always considered the sequoia to be the domain of the Supreme Being and the California forestry department. I don't believe the redwood has been native to this part of the country and its climate and soil conditions in any recent geological epoch. However, consider where it grows in the Pacific Northwest; I assume it requires rich, moist soil, relatively mild winters, and if you want it to grow straight and tall, full sun with no competition from surrounding trees. Plant it and jump back. In four or five hundred years, you will really have something there.

Next time ... sending your orchids off to summer vacation

RADICAL PRUNINGS

JUNE 14

Gardening Advice by Mertensia Corydalis

STIR-FRY THIS!

Q: Dear Mertensia, we've discovered garlic chives in the Chinese grocery store. What a fabu stir-fry ingredient! Can the ordinary home gardener grow these? Also, for your information. Melisande is a mason, in case you ever need some stonework done.
—*Lana and Melisande, North Campus*

A: You are correct, the garlic chive is a wonderful herb, little known to most Americans except those who grow the plants for their handsome white flowers. The leaves are flat, about eight inches to ten inches long, and have the flavor of garlic and onions. You have probably discovered the blanched version, which is a pale straw color, very pungent, and very perishable. Once you locate a source of live plants (you can grow from seed, but it will take a year to get anywhere with them), plant in humus-rich garden soil. Do not be too greedy in cutting leaves until the plants are well established. To blanch, plant them in a trench and keep hilling up the earth as the plants grow. The Chinese have special cylindrical clay pots with lids which they place over the plants in order to blanch the leaves. You can improvise something similar. You must alternate years of blanching and cutting green so the plants can regain their strength.

On the subject of masonry: Yes, I would like to investigate the cost of a stone wall. I seem to have a neighbor who continually violates the space under my fence, spraying with poisons and lopping off plants with a string trimmer.

❧❧❧

Q. Mlle. Corydalis, at the Philadelphia Flower Show, you were so kind to sign my copy of your monograph on bypass pruners. I attended the workshop on garden accoutrements given by you and M. Norton Doyle of *Gracious Way Magazine*. Thank you for your defense of the French mud shoe in the face of M. Doyle's irrational promotion of the British Wellington boot. I found M. Doyle's chauvinism most offensive. —*Catherine, Paris*

A. Dear Catherine, I marvel that your schedule of cinema projects permits you time for the pursuit of gardening. I must also apologize for Mr. Doyle's (my former husband, by the way) unfortunate reference to frogs. There is *un aspect mauvais* to garden journalism that is best not aired before the public.

❧❧❧

Q. Miss Mertensia, since you show such disdain for answering your readers' lawn-care questions, allow me to suggest a new book, *Perfect Lawns for Morons*. Please consider recommending it to your readers. —*Ralph, Bienvue*

A. This paperback was prominently displayed in my local bookstore. How could one miss it, the cover being of bold yellow and black design, like the Cliffs Notes I used to crib on John Milton at university. It has such topics as "Creative Mowing" and "You Can Win the Quack Grass War." I did consider it for what the computer people call a nanosecond (in garden time, one beat of a hummingbird's wings). I think the title says it all.

Readers, any of you who are curling up with a book on lawncare need to reexamine the meaning of your lives.

Next time ... brassica pests ... the buzz on the new bee balms

RADICAL PRUNINGS
SPECIAL ISSUE

A READERS SURVEY

Dear Readers,

A weeding session offers the gardener the opportunity to target a previously overlooked space in which yet another plant can be added to your collection, to explore possibilities for a dinner party menu, and to review all your grievances with the local politicians. Recently, while plucking the germinations of seeds blown in from the gardens of careless neighbors, my mind wandered to an exploration of how this column can be improved, how can it be more informative, how can it be, as Miss Vong puts it "your user friend." The answers lie, of course, in what you have to tell me about yourself. Inspired by the ladies' magazine quizzes so beloved by Miss Vong ("Are You Driving Him Wild? Rate Yourself"), I offer our very first Readers Survey. So get out your No. 2 pencils and have at it.

For fertilizer, I use:

A   composted cow or horse manure
B   bat guano or "hot" chicken manure
C   chemical fertilizers

My parterres are edged with:

A buxus, trimmed
B clipped rosemary
C densely planted santolina

When I go on tours of private gardens, I:

A make sketches and notes of ideas to try at home
B chat with the host gardeners about their unusual specimens
C surreptitiously steal rooting slips from their unusual specimens

For my indoor gardening, I have:

A a bay window greenhouse
B a solarium
C a free-standing greenhouse
D an orangerie/conservatory

To deal with Japanese beetles, I:

A pluck them off plants and drown them in a pail of benzene
B spray them with chemical poisons
C collect and release them near the property of some unpleasant person

The ultimate vision of my own garden is:

A a lushly planted English-style cottage garden
B Zen-inspired precision of understatement
C a postwar 1950s suburban-style treeless lawn

When I find volunteer (self-sown) plants, I:

A nurture them
B pot them up and share with friends
C rip them out and send them off to the community landfill

In my potager I grow:

A heirloom varieties of fruits and vegetables
B decorative varieties of fruits and vegetables
C bullet-proof varieties of tomatoes bought on sale at Kmart
D I do not have a potager (Please explain why not:

_____

_____

_____

_____)

My annual garden budget is:

A I am not restricted by budget concerns
B $500 to $1000
C I buy my six-pack of impatiens on sale at Kmart

I garden:

A as a solitary pursuit
B with my significant other, bickering the whole time
C with a hired assistant who is willing to go beyond the scope of the garden itself

I learned to garden by:

A observing a parent or grandparent when I was a child

B extensive reading and trial and error

C allowing a talented hired assistant to have his head

My age level is:

A child to young adult

B 30s to 40s

C not to be spoken of

I would like more information about:

A floraculture

B hardscaping

C the inside "dish" on the hort world

D other (Specify: _____

_____

_____)

There you have it, dear Readers. Feel free to add your comments, but remember to be polite. You will notice that the form is not postage-paid. You will have to get your responses back to me at your own expense. Miss Mertensia has to stand the cost of having her staff (Miss Vong) tabulate and analyze the results. You are reminded that our subscription price has not kept apace with increases in postage costs, paper supplies, etc., etc.

Next time ... taking advantage of sports of Nature

SUMMER

RADICAL PRUNINGS

JUNE 21

Gardening Advice by Mertensia Corydalis

JUNE—A BIRTHDAY TOAST TO THE MARQUIS

Q. My hosta have a number of holes in the leaves. I can't see any bugs on them. What is doing this, and what can I do about it? —*Phyllis, Lewiston*

A. The holes were chewed by slugs, which do their work at night, retiring to the underside of wood mulch or rocks during the day. There are poison granules available, but you don't want a curious animal to nibble on them. You may surround each plant with a copper wire, which will electrocute the snail when it crawls over the wire. Save that method for the sadists and social conservatives among us. Instead, set out saucers of beer among the hosta plants. Not your craft-brewed porters and ales, but cheap, mass-produced canned beer. The slugs, a belly-scratching lot, will be distracted on their way to work by your tavern on the green. In the morning: stiff as boards. Dump the lot on your compost heap and start over again. This method will amuse any children (who are natural-born sadists, by the way) you might have and can be turned into an instructive example of the consequences of immoderate consumption of alcohol. I hope your hostas are enjoying a shaded area. I am seeing these plants stuck all over the place, struggling in the hot sun next to concrete driveways.

❧❧❧❧

Q. Dear Miss Mertensia, a friend gave me a small Venus flytrap as a get-well gift while I was in rehab. How do I take care of it? Do I need to feed it insects? Can I get it to grow quite large by using, say, Wunda-Gro? —*Dick, Near North*

A. The Venus flytrap is a bog-dwelling plant, so you must keep it under warm, humid conditions and in bright, indirect light. A terrarium would be ideal. This can be an unused fishbowl or any deep, clear glass bowl, with a glass plate for a removable cover. Please consult a library book on how to plant a terrarium, as space does not permit here. I once saw a very interesting collection of carnivorous plants being cultivated outdoors in a countersunk child's wading pool filled with soil and sphagnum moss. If your plant needed chemical fertilizer, Wunda-Acid, rather than Wunda-Gro, would be appropriate. However, if you get the potting medium right, no artificial feeding is needed, as the plant takes in its nutrients through the root system. An occasional insect, which is slowly dissolved and digested by enzymes released in the throat of the plant, is merely an *amuse-gueule*. If it will help speed your recovery, you may entertain the plant and yourself by feeding it a stray housefly.

꙳꙳꙳

DID YOU KNOW?

Hosta and arum leaves, cut and added to your floral arrangements, are long-lasting, lend a variety of shape and texture, and fill up a lot of space when blooms are too dear or too few.

Next time… contorted filberts … staking your belladonna

RADICAL PRUNINGS

JUNE 27

Gardening Advice by Mertensia Corydalis

STEAMED BUNS

Dear Readers,

In response to the many inquiries about Miss Vong, there will not be a little Vong in the immediate future. Let's just say it was all a mistaken conclusion (too many haricot-vert paste sweets enjoyed over the Tet holidays), and let it go at that. However, we will not be too hasty in returning the layette items the readers bestowed on Miss Vong. The last we heard of Mr. Troung he was shrimping off the coast of Louisiana. There is now a Mr. Binh, confectionery manager of the Hanoi Hut Grocery and Carry-out, who takes our Miss Vong (in red lipstick and platform shoes) discoing nightly.

How I envy the energy of the young! On weekends, Miss Vong does duty as receptionist at her girlfriends' You've Got Nails salon, in which she has invested her modest savings. Everything seems to be okay these days for Miss Vong.

Today I noticed that a stand-up cardboard automobile has been added to the gallery on Miss Vong's desk.

Q. Miss Corydalis, watering the garden takes so much time, and I'm never sure how much it really needs. I think we should install an irrigation system with drip emitters and a timer. My husband says we can't afford it and that it's adequate for him to go out every evening and water the garden by hand. What is your opinion? —*Pia, Marmot Hollow*

A. Pia, it's been my experience that husbands, who normally leap at any opportunity to invest in gadgetry, love to spend the twilight of the day, hose in hand, lost in solitary reverie. So to keep the peace, perhaps you should defer. The only danger is that frequent, shallow watering encourages root growth near the soil surface, leaving the plant vulnerable during periods of intense heat. This summer is already unusually hot. Just today I had to insist that Tran remove his shirt to avoid overheating while dividing my veronica.

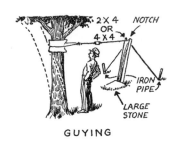

GUYING

NEW TO OUR CATALOGUE:

Artisan-woven **WILLOW FOOTSTOOLS** for your porch or sun room. No returns if your footstool sprouts during humid weather. A steal at $59.00!

CHESTNUT TUTEURS: nothing but the best for your sweet peas' needy clambering. Write your support check now. $79.00 each, but, dear Readers, they'll last forever.

Next time ... updating your pergola

RADICAL PRUNINGS

JULY 5

Gardening Advice by Mertensia Corydalis

FROM THE TERRACE

Dear Readers,

I have banished myself, in yellow mackintosh, to the terrace on this dreary, drizzling day to compose today's column by hand on legal pad. Jasper and Jennelle are huddled under the table. Due to your overwhelming response to the Readers Survey, Miss Vong, who is tabulating the results, has piles of printouts on every surface. Moreover, she has taken to listening to her favorite rap music group, Phat Maudit, in the office. The thumping vibrations caused a Limoges teacup to leap to its death. The widowed saucer has been demoted to status of ashtray by Miss Vong and her newest bad habit.

Some of you took the trouble to fax me a copy of *Newsworthy Magazine*'s interview with Norton Doyle (my former husband) on the subject of virtual gardening. Believe me, it had not escaped my attention. In the article, Doyle referred to me as Mertensia "rip-out-your-lawn-and-lower-the-property-value" Corydalis, an example of the low-tech gardener of the past. That's from a man who requires defibrillation at the sight of a stray autumn leaf scudding across his lawn. Well, any of you who get distressed over a little dirt under your fingernails, I guess you can just sit basking in the glow of your computer screen and garden away for all I care. That's fewer chain saws, leaf blowers, and riding mowers for the rest of us to endure.

Tran was busy all morning in the potting shed, whetting spades and trowels and washing a basket of freshly dug red shallots. Then he left in his little pick-up truck for a soccer game with fellow gardeners.

I don't know what I shall do when the weather turns cooler. I suppose I will have to provide a set of headphones and an environmental purifier for Miss Vong. In her defense I must say that Miss Vong types at rocket speed, and what she lacks in English syntax, she makes up with ferocious instinct for the hunt with the spell-checking program.

A garden in the rain recovers from the constant, intrusive fussing by human hand. The flowers (except for the blues: the cerulean heads of Nikko hydrangea and the saturated electric lobelia) recede in the cool light, and the variation in hue and texture of the foliage is seen with a new clarity.

> *Dear Highly Estimated Friends, Miss Mertensia is having migraine and having to lie down. She ask me to result the Reader Survey. I am working on it, OK? Also I am to reminding you, lawn-care questions not allowed. Ever.*
>
> *Your humiliated servant,*
> *Francine Vong*

RADICAL PRUNINGS

JULY 11

Gardening Advice by Mertensia Corydalis

SUNFLOWERS

Dear Readers,

Our rock-star client hosted what can only be described as a bash to celebrate the completion of his new garden. The guests were a lot more colorful than the sort one usually meets at these events. Our standard garden party uniform, floral print voile frock with linen bolero, seemed hopelessly out of step in a sea of spandex and lamé. Miss Vong, becoming very Dom Perignon–compliant as she flitted from celebrity to celebrity, landed at the dessert table where she was hand-fed *petits gateaux* by Herr Rubric, Chef to the Stars. This would not sit well with Mr. Binh, who has indicated he would like to supply Miss Vong with sweets for the rest of her life. She, however, says they must wait for a letter from Uncle Vu, the Vietnamese astrologer, who is to determine if their stars are properly aligned. I believe they have been waiting for quite some time. There is no faxing of Destiny.

As the afternoon wore on, an Amazonian trio of backup singers, in thigh-high boots and rubber minidresses, who bill themselves as Anthony's Trollopes, formed a conga line with my garden assistant Tran and snaked through the garden paths until they disappeared from view. A bit annoying in my opinion. As a member of the design team, he should make himself available to answer any technical questions guests might ask.

Our client urged your Miss Mertensia to join him in a few choruses of…I can't name the song without revealing our client's identity. We have been known to hit a few high notes from time to time, so we said, "Oh, what the hell," and doffed our bolero. My younger readers might be dismayed to learn that the Big Cheese is actually a year older than I (and needs stronger reading glasses, I might add). Our duet lasted a good twenty minutes, during which the Big Cheese remained admirably vertical, and garnered rousing cheers and applause.

Before I bid my host adieu, I took him aside to remind him of his new responsibility. He perked up and seemed to have a moment of lucidity at the mention of deadheading, but there was a bit of disappointment when he was informed that we do not administer spankings to naughty clients who fail to keep gardens well maintained. (Miss Mertensia does not own any leather garments other than Father's wartime RAF navigator's jacket.) A languishing garden is punishment enough.

We did a little high-flying and navigating of our own. Der Grosse Kaese hired a crane with a basket to hoist us high in the air to have a good overview of the garden, as well as to impress the guests. I tried to take a few final photos, but our client was a little woozy from the heat and the altitude, not to mention excessive party refreshments, and I had to grab the back of his belt several times to keep him from toppling out, as we moved slowly across the landscape like a brontosaurus with a rock star struggling in its jaws.

(Note to Larry, the entertainment lawyer from the party who wants to package and franchise me: yes, we'll do lunch. Sometime.)

Q. Dear Mertensia, I planted sunflower seeds two months ago, and the plants are spindly and only about ten inches tall. I see other people's huge sunflowers starting to form flower heads. What could be the problem? —*Marlowe, Hamford*

A. Dear "Marlowe," please sit down, as I have a rude shock for you. Your miniature-picket-fence-enclosed country vignette of sunflower seeds planted in tidy rows, with about three inches between each plant, lies under the canopy of two very large maple trees. Consider a possible correlation between the name "sunflower" and their requirement of sunny exposure in order to grow. I know, you'll dismiss this as menopausal ranting, so I will have to send Tran over with a couple of bottles of ice-cold Singha beer to convince you. The cost of this will be his having to listen again to how your platoon saved an entire village of his countrymen. This, though we know very well the closest you've been to Asia is the package of frozen egg rolls you bought by mistake, thinking they were pizza rolls, and which you magnanimously offered to Miss Vong in hopes of landing your first date in a decade.

Just out of curiosity, why is your mother still coming over every week to mow your lawn at least two years after you had your plantar warts removed?

And finally, Miss Vong has provided me with some early results from the Readers Survey:

— I'm spotting a real trend from your interest in constructing a grotto as a do-it-yourself project.

— An astonishing 40 percent of you want to know if Norton Doyle, garden editor of *Gracious Way Magazine* (and my former husband) prefers annuals, biennials, or perennials. The answer: Yes.

— To a Mr. Candide who asked me to recommend a brand of rotary tiller: Miss Corydalis infrequently reviews large power equipment. I refer you to the Web site of Norton Doyle at www.graciousway hamford.com/nortonstool.

— To Lois of Dudley and the many ladies' garden club members who inquired about the credentials of my garden assistant: Tran has a certificate in horticulture and landscape drafting from the General Tuy Lycée des Jardins and enjoyed extensive practical experience in the private garden of a Frenchwoman in Ho Chi Minh City.

Next time ... hemerocallis—diploids or triploids—what does it all mean?

RADICAL PRUNINGS

JULY 19

Gardening Advice by Mertensia Corydalis

WHAT'S EATING NELSON'S ZUCCHINI?

Q: Dear Mertensia, we're so relieved that you are back. We heard rumors that you had been lost in a ballooning accident. Our zucchini vines are suddenly turning mushy, the leaves wilting and dying. Help! —*Nelson and Bob, Mt. Ashford*

A: Dear Nelson and Bob, the ballooning mishap has been greatly exaggerated, as frequently happens in the society column of the *Hamford Cornet*. There was a sudden downdraft and I lost a very nice hat to the prevailing winds, but we recovered our altitude quickly. On your zucchini: I want all of you out there to close your eyes and conjure up the flavor of zucchini in your mind. Now try to describe it. Can't do it, can you? Now, why did you plant a vegetable that has no flavor, reaches behemoth proportions if not plucked off the vine in its infancy, and which, in the end, no one wants? You will find yourself collecting recipes for zucchini muffins and chocolate zucchini cake, sending your partner off to the office with loaves of zucchini bread to give away. But to answer your question, the vines are being destroyed from the inside by the larva of the squash vine borer. You might save some of the plants by applying a *Bacillus thuringiensis kurstaki* dust, which is a bacteria that destroys the larvae, but not you or good insects like ladybugs. More effective is to purchase a hypodermic syringe and inject a solution of the Btk into the stalk of the vine (but do you really want to face a pharmacist with this cock-and-bull story?).

Or, you can do nothing. Just yank out the plants, sneak them into the rubbish bin (don't spread the problem to your compost pile), and your friends and colleagues will stop avoiding you all summer.

From our Reader Survey (still being compiled and analyzed):

— To a Mr. Peter Volatile, who writes that he grows his tomatoes and other crops in bulletproof containers: Oh, what is the world coming to, when the gardener in the urban courtyard potager must arm his vegetables? For those of you also under siege, the reader advises that Kmart carries a line of Kevlar pots with adequate drainage.

— A reader informs us that Starbucks coffee shops have a policy of making their used grounds available, free of charge, to gardeners (which you can add to your compost or apply directly to the soil surrounding acid-loving plants). I would imagine most other coffee shops would be happy to oblige you. It can't hurt to ask.

— A science-minded Maribeth sent in a schematic for composting pet waste with gazing balls. It involves some complicated geometry and refraction of light—too technical for Miss Corydalis. Just bury the business in your garden away from the edible plants—oh don't act so shocked, your cat and all his friends are already doing it wherever they damned well please.

Next time ... make a hypertufa trough for your alpines

RADICAL PRUNINGS

JULY 26

Gardening Advice by Mertensia Corydalis

THE DEERSLAYER

Q: Dear Mertensia, we saw pea shoots among the produce in an Oriental grocery store. How do you use them and can we grow them in our late summer garden? —*Olivia and Bettina, North Campus*

A: Bettina seems to be a bit of a tumbleweed. I believe I recognize the name from previous queries. To answer your questions about pea shoots or *dou miao*, they are quite a delicacy, which is why they were rather expensive in the grocery store. They are the tender leaves and stems of young snow pea plants. Sow the pea seeds very closely and harvest the shoots often.

They can be eaten raw in salads or just barely wilted in stirfry with ginger, rice wine, and a pinch of sugar. I commented to a Chinese friend, whose family name coincidentally is Miao, which means "shoot" or "sprout," that I found eating the tendrils disagreeable, akin to trying to swallow a hair. She said, "Oh, we pinch them off." Sometimes the perfectly obvious eludes us.

A number of fellow gardeners have recommended Olivia as a certified arborist. Do give me a ring. Tran, my garden assistant, tells me I could use some high-altitude pruning.

It is often inconvenient for Tran to drop what he is doing and drive Miss Vong to the post office or to the groomer for Jasper and Jennelle's baths, so it was decided that Miss Vong would learn to drive her brother Tran's little truck. (I fear my Buick Roadmaster is more than Miss Vong can handle, though the dogs love to ride in "the flying sofa.")

Miss Vong was seated on both the white and yellow pages of the telephone directory in order to see over the steering wheel. Jasper, Jennelle, and I were positioned alongside the driveway to watch the first driving lesson, and we cheered on Miss Vong as the truck lurched past us in first gear. Miss Vong disappeared from view momentarily in order to reach the clutch and graduate to second gear. Despite Tran's frantic shouting, the truck plunged into a stand of artemisia "Powis Castle."

The radiator was impaled on the antlers of a bronze leaping stag. All fell silent, even Jasper and Jennelle. Then Buddha toppled off the dashboard. Steam exploded from under the truck's bonnet. Tran, pounding on the roof of the truck with his fist, cried that he would like to wring Francine's little neck like a chicken and shouted some other much ruder-sounding words that I don't know. Miss Vong was provoked, amidst her sobs, into returning some rude-sounding language of her own. Jasper and Jennelle joined the fray with enthusiastic barking. I had to go lie down for a while before dealing with the insurance people regarding the bronze stag and, oh yes, the truck, now referred to as the Deerslayer.

GLEANINGS

Artemisia annua, Sweet Annie or Qing guo, has long been used in China as a medicinal herb. Toxic to the malaria parasite, it is now the main component of antimalarial drugs, which are replacing the older quinine preparations.

Next time ... new trends in mulching ... shopping for rocks

RADICAL PRUNINGS

AUGUST 2

Gardening Advice by Mertensia Corydalis

DON'T GET YOUR ASTERS IN A BIND

Dear Readers,

Tormented by guilt.

That's how I want you to be. I want you to be so Catholic you will mount a crucifix on the prow of your Lawnboy. Every time you run a potassium-rich banana peel through the garbage disposal instead of adding it to your compost pile, I want you to be so wracked by guilt that even an hour in the confessional won't fix it. Make it a habit. You will feel the flames of Hell licking at your ankles if you dare put your grapefruit rinds in the rubbish bin. Figure out how to make your composting system so easy you won't give it a second thought. Finished compost is something you cannot buy, and no one will share it with you. Even your own mother wouldn't give you a shovelful if it would save your very life. Brace yourself for frequent tirades on this subject!

Q. Dear Mertensia, my late summer garden is looking pretty tired. What are some flowering perennials I can put in now?
—*Randolph, Buck Run*

A. Randolph, asters (whose name derives from the Greek and Latin for "star") are the very plants to fill the bill. They are widely available in late summer and put on their show in September, some up to hard frost. The color range is white, pinks, purples, and bluish reds. They require little care, although a few varieties are prone to powdery mildew. Read the labels for ultimate height. It is very important to locate asters according to their height as they are not an attractive plant until they begin to flower. In fact, provide permanent labels for them, because it is easy to mistake them for weeds earlier in the year. You may need to stake the taller varieties, using four bamboo pea sticks, weaving garden twine around the sticks and through the stalks. Do not corset them; allow them some languid flopping over—they are, after all, a shower of little stars.

❧❧❧❧

Q. Dear Miss Mertensia, I am receiving some very tempting mail order offers for lily bulbs. I would like to make a mass planting, so price is an issue. —*Dee, Doe Run*

A. Just as there is no such thing as leftover lobster, there is no such thing as too many lilies in the garden. The ad you sent to me is from a mail-order company which specializes in suspicious oddities like twenty-five-foot-tall tomato plants, winter-hardy banana trees, bifurcated cucumbers, and so on. The bulbs they offer may well be undersized culls. Go with a reputable company, consider your color scheme, and order as many as you can afford (and beyond). Immediately remove the bulbs you purchase from any plastic packaging and place in marked paper bags or you will lose them to mold. Plant the lilies as soon as possible (tulips, daffodils, etc., can wait), the tall trumpets in the back of the bed, stargazers in mid bed, and shorter Asiatic lilies near the front, giving bone meal and compost to all.

Here is a florist's tip: when you cut lilies to bring in for bouquets, remove the anthers. These are usually black or yellow, teetering at the top of the thin stalks surrounding the center of the lily. They are the male part of the flower, and the sperm-bearing pollen can badly stain tablecloths and the flowers themselves. You are, in effect, gelding the lily.

Next time ... feeling Gaudi? Make a *picassiette* wall

RADICAL PRUNINGS

AUGUST 10

Gardening Advice by Mertensia Corydalis

SUNFLOWERS REDUX

Q. Dear Mertensia, some of my sunflowers turned out great— over seven feet tall. The problem is that for more than half the day the flowers themselves are facing my neighbor's yard, so I can't enjoy them. Are you supposed to orient the seeds a certain way to prevent this? I feel cheated out of all my hard work. My neighbor is getting something for nothing! —*Herrick, Hamford*

A. Dear "Herrick," we're really reaching into the Bin of Literary Obscurity for our pseudonyms now, aren't we? The reason your neighbor (as if I'm in such a fog I didn't recognize myself) is enjoying your surviving sunflowers (transplanted from a shaded location) is that they are heliotropic plants, focusing on the sun as we travel around it in the course of the day. Since my property is on your south side, the sunflowers are craning their necks in my direction during most of the day, casting their faces down in resignation as they prepare to spend the evening facing your side of the fence. I saw you out there trying to "adjust" them. Some people are so territorial, I'm surprised they aren't out lifting their legs to the surveyor's pins, marking their little parcel of turf.

— 103 —

Q: We are performance artists—perhaps you have heard about our presentation, in which we emerge, nude, from suspended black rubber chrysalides, wet with the vernix caseosa of newborns (actually fat-free lemon chiffon yogurt), interpret our life cycles through dance, and perish consuming each other in the act of love. We would like our garden to really make a statement. Can you suggest some out-of-the-ordinary plants? —*Andre and Agathe, borgne.confondre@hamford.net*

A: Those of you for whom passing out bite-size Milky Way candy bars one night a year is not sufficient observance of Halloween might be interested in a special area of my own garden. This small space, the Charles Baudelaire Memorial Garden, is anchored by a contorted hazelnut tree and a broken Doric column. I have made a little hobby of collecting the nearest-to-black plants that I can find. Some of the specimens include: *Ophiopogon planiscapus* "nigrescens" (black mondo grass), hemerocallis Black Magic, a Black Jade miniature rose, Ink Spots and Taboo hybrid tea roses, Superstition bearded iris, black *Alcea rosea* (hollyhocks), and pansies as deep and velvety as a party dress (and Jennelle's ears). Here is a tip: dark reds seem to be optically closer to black than dark blues and purples. In the future I hope to add a pleurant, an eternally mourning statue such as is found in French graveyards.

Miss Vong has requested that I purchase new spreadsheet and database programs (whatever those are), as she is falling behind in tabulating the Readers Survey. You have been clamoring to know the results. Patience.

COOKERY

Oh, the howls of protest received from zucchini lovers for my opinion of the vegetable in a recent newsletter. And the recipes: battered and deep-fried; hollowed out into pirogues and stuffed with everything from tuna-fish casserole to ground-buffalo sloppy joes; even made into a sorbet! I thought my readership was a little more…well…you know. I will reveal my one zucchini dish, saved for when I just can't deal with any vegetable that requires more preparation: slice baby zucchini, no more than about six inches long, thinly. Arrange on a lightly olive-oiled shallow dish. Sprinkle with finely chopped garlic, rosemary leaves (or any herbal combination you have growing), salt and pepper, another drizzle of olive oil, and roast in a four-hundred-degree oven until lightly browned and almost crisp, perhaps ten minutes. That's it.

I still maintain the zucchini is just a vehicle for the other flavors.

Next time … a sedum for every season

RADICAL PRUNINGS

AUGUST 22

Gardening Advice by Mertensia Corydalis

NAKED BOYS AND THE SPORTING LIFE

Q. Last fall I planted a caryopteris "Blue Mist." I was very disappointed that it did not bloom this year. In fact, the top growth, while healthy, was pretty sparse. What am I doing wrong?
—*Roland, Montrose*

A. Dear Roland, I am guessing that you did not cut the woody stems back to the ground in late winter. This encourages vigorous new growth on which the flowers are carried. Try it with a light feeding in the spring and see if you don't have happy results. Happily, I have not found this radical pruning to my own caryopteris necessary for a number of years. A small shrub, this is a splendid plant, with silver foliage and sky blue flowers that bloom well into autumn. It brought great joy to the bees and butterflies when I added a specimen to my Blue Bed (you know by now that Miss Corydalis loves monochromatic plantings). This area includes salvia, lavender, columbine, and *Tradescantia*. I am thinking of edging the front of the bed with cobalt blue mineral-water bottles, turned upside down. Tran says I'm crazy, and that he'll have to continually wipe dust and mud off them. What do you think?

Q. Our local nursery has fall-blooming bulbs for sale. Neither of us has ever seen them in a garden. What can you tell us?

—*Nelson and Bob, Mt. Ashford*

A. When touring a public garden on a warm October day, I once saw the arresting combination of the popular lavender PJM azalea in bloom, with pink Naked Boys (colchium) at its feet. I asked the head groundskeeper if the azalea had been forced indoors. He assured me that that the variety sometimes reblooms in the fall after a few weeks of not-quite-freezing nights. Colchium and the smaller (and much less expensive) *C. speciosus* and *C. sativus* are saffron crocuses. (Yes, culinary saffron.) They are small blooms on short stems, so you should remove fallen tree leaves carefully by hand or you may miss them entirely. They may not have time to bloom the first fall so it's well to mark where you plant them. The larger colchiums are called Naked Boys because they will bloom without soil. Just set the bulbs on a windowsill and enjoy their delicate rosiness close up. Plant them out after the flowers are spent.

Dear Readers,

I don't recall exactly how I got talked into this, and I barely remember writing a check for the printed shirts, but it seems I am now the sponsor of Tran's soccer team, the Miltonhurst Mulching Machine. This past Sunday the Ladies' Wisteria Study Group had a date to tour an arboretum. Instead we piled into my Buick Roadmaster with lawn chairs, a picnic basket of finger sandwiches and éclairs, a giant thermos of wine punch, and off we went to cheer on the Mulching Machine as it played the Hibiscus Farms Hybridizers. Tran, in his little shorts and long black silk hair tied back in a samurai's chignon, carried the day. Too bad only one in our club remotely understands the game. We had planned to attend a lecture on dormant pruning next Sunday, but the Machine has a match with the Metro Botanical Conservatory Curators. We're there.

Next time ... the news about yews ... what's hot in spring bulbs

RADICAL PRUNINGS

SEPTEMBER 3

Gardening Advice by Mertensia Corydalis

THE YOUNG PEACH BARES HER ROOTS

Dear Readers:

The excitement is building here at Miltonhurst. There has been a flurry of faxes and e-mails, conventional letters with snapshots, and expensive telephone calls back and forth between here and China. A long-awaited package is on its way.

This quest began years ago when Miss Mertensia was a graduate assistant to a famous ethnobotanist, the late Dr. Lewis Z Greenleaf. Young and impressionable, I toiled under Lewis Z. while on a collecting expedition in the wilds of western Szechuan Province. Poor Lewis Z.'s nerves were shot from almost having been in the Bataan Death March, and he frequently—well, usually—remained in camp, calming himself with a beaker of well-aged Shaoxing, while I clung to rocky hillsides, uprooting specimens of *Rosa sericea*, some bearing inch-long thorns.

While traipsing around China, Lewis Z. introduced me to Chen Xie Lin, a master breeder of tree peonies. Overwhelmed by the beauty of his creations, I resolved that someday when I had my own garden, I would make one of his tree peonies the star. Master Lin and his enchanted garden seemed to drop off the edge of the earth during the Cultural Revolution, when it was forbidden to cultivate flowers only for their pleasure. Now, with months of detective work and a labyrinth of paperwork and bribery by my daughter Astrid, who represents Amelia Faye Beauty Products in China, the Reclining Young Peach is on her way.

Q: Dear Miss Corydalis, we bought a Brown Turkey fig tree at a late-summer nursery sale. Now the question is, how do we winter it over? It is still in the nursery pot, as we are not sure of the best way to plant it. —*Mel and Judith, Beechwood*

A: Even though you bought one of the hardiest varieties available, I still recommend treating the fig as a container plant in this climate, at least until spring, when the tree can establish itself in the ground over an entire growing season. Use a humus-y garden soil, with a spadeful of lime in the pot. Tran must have a Sicilian chromosome in his genes. For years I tried to winter over fig trees, trying all the prescriptions given me by elderly Italian gentlemen: I've tried caging in burlap stuffed with straw, bowing the branches over, tethering them to the ground and heaping the tree over with leaves, then wrapping in burlap, potting, and storing in an unheated enclosed porch, and so on. None made it to year two or three, when one could expect the happy appearance of figlets. But, this past November, Tran cut the latest potted tree back to soil level and slipped the pot into a huge cardboard carton stuffed with straw. This was watered, sealed in its box, and put into the unheated garage. True, we had a mild winter, which certainly helped. With the arrival of April, we brought the pot out into the sunlight and were surprised to find many green, foot-long budded shoots. The tree was transplanted into the ground, sited near the potting shed wall, where it is sheltered from our harsh weather-bearing southwestern winds. At the beginning of September, there were a half dozen ripe figs and we enjoyed them right there in the garden until the juices ran down our chins. Tran is a genius!

On the advice of the concrete contractor who repaired my driveway, we have purchased a special concrete insulating blanket from a builders' supply house and will wrap the fig this year after the first serious frost. Mr. Antonelli assures us we will be sick of figs by the end of next September.

COOKERY

A delicious way to enjoy your figs is to cut a slit in the side of each fat fig and insert a bit of gorgonzola cheese. Heat the figs on a baking tray until the cheese is barely melted. Arrange the very warm figs on a platter lined with some leaves from your fig tree (hydrangea leaves will do if you got your figs from the greengrocer). A perfect hors d'oeuvre to pass around at your next party.

One of these is not enough. Two are not quite enough. Eat three and you're beginning to make a spectacle of yourself.

Next time ... welcoming your orchids home from summer vacation

RADICAL PRUNINGS

SEPTEMBER 12

Gardening Advice by Mertensia Corydalis

THE HUNT OF THE RED ADMIRAL

Miss Mertensia was catching up on a stack of gossip newspapers and enjoying the Philip Glass recording of *Mishima* when she noticed Jennelle intently watching a movement near the ceiling. A red admiral butterfly had found its way into the house. I tried to capture it in the only thing handy, which was a high-crowned straw hat. The frantic beating of the red admiral's wings pulsed in time to the galloping notes of the "Runaway Horses" movement. Jennelle gravely followed me around the room as I swooped the hat time and time again in futility. Finally the red admiral, exhausted, came to rest against a kitchen windowpane, where I trapped it with a strawberry basket and a piece of stiff paper slid between the basket and the glass. I took a moment to admire his wings, like a samurai's black *montsuki* with red bands and white family crests on the sleeves. It is time for the red admiral's migration. After releasing it and returning to my chaise, I began to wonder that I don't own a butterfly net, having just about every other little-used object imaginable. (Mishima was a Japanese novelist and political eccentric who brought his brief life to an end by committing seppuku, ritual disemboweling.)

Q. A lawn-care company is offering me a contract which includes a light feeding and application of weed killer now and a spraying in late autumn to prevent snow mold. Is the second treatment worthwhile? —*Hernando, Hideway Hills*

A. Dear Hernando, obviously you are a new reader, and if you wish to continue being a reader of this column, you must be aware of two things: (1) we do not entertain lawn-care questions and (2) we disapprove of gratuitous herbicide and pesticide spraying. If Miss Vong were not so consumed with tabulating the results of the Readers Survey, she would have intercepted your letter. (Miss Vong has ordered a scanning machine, which she claims will enable her to pass the survey forms through to get instant results). Just this morning a lawn-care company's poison truck pulled up to my door. The driver, in nonpermeable uniform and heavy rubber boots suitable for working in a Soviet nuclear power plant, offered me a deal which would give a me significant discount for scheduling a spraying at the same time as all my neighbors. The readers know what a gentle soul I usually am, but let's just say there was a meltdown in my foyer and that particular driver will not be at my door again. I need not fret about providing for my old age, surrounded as I am by clouds of carcinogens.

❧❧❧

Q. I just started composting this year, and when I finally took a shovelful from the bottom, a pretty dazed mouse staggered out and disappeared under a nearby woodpile. I was afraid a compost bin would attract vermin, and sure enough, it did. Can I put some mouse bait in the bin? —*Mikhail, souris@cheeznet.net*

A: No you may not. Now let me get this straight: you want to put a product in your compost that will cause a mammal to die of a massive internal hemorrhage? You have mice in your compost. Live with it. As a matter of fact, it's an ideal spot for a winter nest—warm, safe, and providing plenty for the brood to eat when they're off mother's milk. And if you have ever found evidence of mice in your pantry, you know that the output equals the input, so the mice are doing some work for you.

Lots of things are going on in your garden that you don't know about and which are pretty much none of your business. I hope the mouse recovered from his concussion. Nature is tough enough without you contributing human cruelty to it.

Next time ... reflect the sky with a rill

RADICAL PRUNINGS

SEPTEMBER 26

Gardening Advice by Mertensia Corydalis

TWO POINTS ON THE COLOR WHEEL

Dear Readers,

Today Tran insisted that I hop into his truck. There was something he had seen on his way to work that he wanted to show me. He drove to a modest part of town where a lamppost in a front yard was smothered in a mass of morning glories, the intensely blue trumpets as big as saucers. At the base, a stand of bright goldenrod (solidago). I have a bias against morning glory because of our never-ending battle with bindweed, but I have to admit this is one of the happiest, and simplest, plantings you could imagine. Just two plants, one of them probably a wildling at that. It was a worthwhile excursion.

Q. Dear Miss Corydalis, I never miss your columns even though I don't really have a garden. Being very busy with my career as an interpretive dancer, I can only manage a few indoor plants. I have a very large fern which used to hang in a previous place of my employment. It's dropping leaves like crazy, really making a mess. I know ferns need humidity and I keep it watered and misted. Can you help? Also, someone told me that a loyal member of my audience named Nortie is related to you. Is that true? —*Acqua Tayne, Hamford*

A. Dear Ms. Tayne, thank you for being a faithful reader. It's possible that you are over-watering the fern. The misting is a good idea—central heating creates a terribly dry environment. Knock the plant out of its pot and take a look at the roots. Since it is a large plant, I suspect it has become pot-bound. If so, tease the roots to loosen them up and repot in a larger container with fresh soil mix and a little all-purpose fertilizer. Speaking of teasing, your audience member Nortie, connoisseur of the arts, sounds like Norton, my former husband. Be careful not to muss his trousers when you are doing your interpreting in his lap. He takes his tweeds very seriously.

૨૨૨૨

Q. Dear Mertensia, we have several flourishing tomato plants in our garden. Can we store unripe tomatoes after the first frost to use for frying? —*Ron and Keeshia, Bienville*

A. Pick blemish-free green tomatoes before they are touched by frost. Choose fruits that are about the size of ripe tomatoes. They will not grow any larger after you pick them. Store them in a cool closet in a tray or box lid lined with several layers of newspaper and covered with a single layer of newspaper. Inspect the fruit every few days and use or discard any fruit which shows signs of rot. Some fruit will eventually ripen—you may even have ripe tomatoes for Thanksgiving! You can accelerate ripening by putting the tomatoes in a paper bag with an apple, which gives off ethylene gas. For frying green, you might want to let the tomatoes get a bit yellow for a more mellow flavor. And of course you can also make a salsa cruda of the fruit at just about any stage.

While in Charleston, South Carolina, for their annual fall garden festival, I enjoyed lunch in the tearoom of an elegant little hotel, where the only sounds were of soft-spoken ladies who lunch and the tinkle of silverware on china. I had a salad of crisp baby spinach dressed with a warm maple-syrup vinaigrette and toasted pecans, topped with cornmeal-crunchy slices of fried green tomatoes, and buttered fingers of date bread on the side. Just recalling the lunch makes me want to head for the kitchen!

Whether you enjoy your tomatoes green or ripened, you will surely miss them when they're gone.

Next time ... those Zen-sational Japanese gardens

AUTUMN

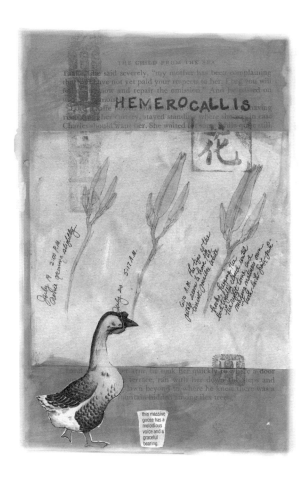

RADICAL PRUNINGS

OCTOBER 2

Gardening Advice by Mertensia Corydalis

THE NEW ARRIVAL

Beyond the Wei
The plain is open and pleasant.
That knight and lady,
Merrily they sport.
Then she gives him a peony.

(Anonymous, *The Book of Odes*, 600 B.C.)

Dear Readers,

Not since Henry, our letter carrier, came to the door of my childhood home with a special delivery for my widowed mother has a postman been greeted with such enthusiasm. The Reclining Young Peach tree peony has arrived.

Nearly a year ago my daughter, Astrid, (well, former husband Norton had a part in this, too, but believe me, it was de minimus) tracked down master tree-peony breeder Chen Xie Lin, sent us photos of his peonies, and afterward Tran and I chose the silky ivory, coral-throated Reclining Young

Peach and negotiated the maze of export permits, packing regulations, and quarantine forms, and paid out a yuan or two here and there to "grease the wheels". But all that comes easily to Astrid, who is responsible for the phenomenal success of Amelia Faye Beauty Products in the People's Republic of China, accomplished by passing out catalogues and moisturizer samples at factory collective meetings, persuading lady party officials that a flick of mascara and a touch of blush would be a great leap forward.

In the meantime, in the garden, it has been like preparing the nursery for a child about to be born. Ever since a suitable location was chosen for planting, Tran has been working on amending the soil, adding lime and testing daily until the pH level reached exactly 6.75, and making a special compost of the spring crop of English pea plants and manure from Osmond, the organically-fed rabbit raised by the little Brownie Scout who lives across the road. As the time of arrival grew closer, we would catch ourselves studying the vacant site, crumbling a little of the soil in our fingers, visualizing the splendid flowers. Daydreaming.

There was a little peony-planting ceremony with lunch of caramelized shrimp and gingered broccoli (the florets graciously left us by our visiting woodchuck) afterward. To make it a foursome, we invited Trooper Ella, who brought Osmond along in a cat transport, much to the entertainment of Jasper and Jennelle.

Q. Dear Miss Corydalis, I have a shady area in my yard, with a tall thicket on one side and a silver maple on the other, where growing grass has been an exercise in futility. I am considering growing shade perennials. Some suggestions please.

—Les, Issmoor

A. Dear Les, congratulations on your wise decision to work with Nature rather than against it. Turn your shady area into a patch of woodland, no matter how small. First, does the thicket need a bit of manicuring? Next, the soil needs to be rich in humus. This fall, shred your leaves and blanket the area with them. By spring they will be virtually decomposed and easily forked into the soil. Do your planning now. Lay out a little path of woodchips. As you drive about, watch for tree-removal crews. You may be able to carry away a small, gnarled stump or a log segment or two for free. If you can talk the crew into cutting a few log slices to lay in your woodchip path, so much the better. Can a bench be fit into your design? Right now, you can put in some spring bulbs—clutches of snowdrops, anenomes (Grecian windflowers), pheasant's eye white narcissus, and fall-blooming cyclamen. You could also put in hellebore (Lenten rose) and tricyrtis (toad lily) this fall. Don't try to get the whole thing planted now. You can place some hostas, ferns, and wild ginger in the spring. My own woodland garden includes my spring-blooming blue-flowered namesakes: mertensia (Virginia bluebells) and corydalis (commonly known as fumewort, which my former husband needs to point out at every opportunity in his writings).

Next time ... last call for mesclun

RADICAL PRUNINGS

OCTOBER 14

Gardening Advice by Mertensia Corydalis

NO ORANGE FLOWERS PLEASE, WE'RE BRITISH

Dear Readers,

As you will recall, back in the spring of this year we announced a contest in which you were invited to get any desire for orange flowers out of your system by planting an all-orange garden and sending pictures and a plant list to be judged by me. I'm sorry, but only in-focus photographs qualified for the competition. (Your impressionistic Polaroids and colored pencil drawings were summarily returned.) Here are the winners:

The **GRAND PRIZE**, a Sheffield steel trowel with rosewood handle (page 2 in the Mertensia Post Haste Catalogue) from our Signature Line of garden accessories, goes to Avid Gardener (he/she prefers to remain anonymous) who came up with a very tricky design of pale apricot digitalis (foxglove), a light orange *papaver somniferum* (opium poppy), and salmon-colored datura (angels-trumpet). Tying it all together is *impomoea batatus* "Blackie," the deeply purple, nearly black-leaved sweet potato vine, allowed to sprawl on the ground. All toxic. All malevolence in the guise of beauty. The trowel, gift-wrapped, of course, is on its way to Avid's post office box.

SECOND PRIZE goes to Lois of Dudley who heeded my clucking over her original desire for a Tropicana rose and exceeded my wildest expectations by setting out a superb kitchen garden which includes orange plum tomatoes, orange bell peppers, butternut squash, and orange nasturtiums and calendulas. Lois is a new gardener who has really "got with the program." I know, most readers presumed that the contest was restricted to orange flowers, but it's my contest, and I'm passing out the prizes. To Lois, the hand-painted tole box of heirloom tomato seed packets (page 12).

THIRD PRIZE goes to Buddy of Rising Creek, who grew from seed what he says is a nearly quarter-acre-solid mass of three-foot-tall orange French marigolds, for the planting's "Take that!" attitude and potential to cause retinal damage by just looking at it. Buddy, there is a pair of lemon yellow rubber garden clogs reserved for you (page 4). Give us a ring with your shoe size.

Q. Dear Mertensia, we've invested quite a bit of money in garden mums. Is there some secret to making them survive the winter and rebloom next year? —*Rex, Westford*

A. The secret is to purchase and plant hardy chrysanthemums back in June and allow them the summer to become well acclimated to their home. The problem is finding a nursery that sells gold or bronze mums in early summer. You will probably have to turn to a mail-order source, which you can find on the Internet. Lacking that foresight (who has bronze-colored mums on his mind in June?), plant the mums as soon as possible, teasing the roots loose if necessary, in a good-size hole. Backfill with very friable soil so the roots won't have to work too hard to grow outward, and most important, water the plants well—and keep them watered well. After a hard frost, cut the plant back to ground level and apply several inches of mulch. Even taking these measures, in a cold climate your chance of success is slim. Resign yourself to the fact that the mums are no more than a splash of color to brighten days that are growing shorter and grayer.

Tran has asked for his Christmas bonus early in order to book a flight home to Vietnam for the lunar new year. He has been in a peevish mood lately, owing probably to the change of season. Sometimes I forget what a young person he is and I take for granted the considerable accomplishment of learning the identity and culture of hundreds of plants not part of his training in tropical flora. Once winter begins to settle upon us, there is little for him to do outdoors and indoors, only an occasional landscape design project (he has a dramatic way with watercolor) and tweaking my phaleonopsis in the solarium. So I am relieved about the trip, because in the past three years he has gone to work during the winter at the Metro Botanical Conservatory in the tropical exhibition area, and there Madame la Directresse has tried to steal him away from me, coveting his talents with hothouse flowers.

Next time ... rating the rakes

RADICAL PRUNINGS

OCTOBER 27

Gardening Advice by Mertensia Corydalis

UNSEASONABLE HEAT WAVE

Dear Readers,

Miss Vong and I began Monday morning oblivious to the storm clouds forming just outside the French doors, which open onto the terrace. We were absorbed in the exacting task of entering the names of at least a hundred varieties of pulmonaria into her spell checker, this for my new book-in-progress on the topic. Even the dogs' restive pacing and nervous glances out the glass doors, those movements prescient of impending electrical storms and earthquakes, went unheeded. So when the French doors burst open with the force of a sudden tempest, we reacted in jaw-dropping astonishment.

Tran, holding the ragged remains of a plant, marched across my pale-rose Aubusson carpet in his muddy wellies. Jasper, with the wisdom attained from a bit of age, retreated to the safety of a spot under the library table. On the other hand, Jennelle, recognizing her handiwork, sat happily tapping her tail on the carpet. Tran gave her a look with black eyes that could have burned holes and called her Chinese dumpling, and if you know anything about certain exotica of Asian cuisine, this was not a term of affection. More specifically,

I think he called her Fukien Chinese dumpling. This just infuriated me—after all, in dog logic, any plant possessing the magic power to command such attention and generate so much happiness is worthy of a revisit.

Putting criminal allegations aside for the moment, I had a few remarks regarding the carpet. Moreover, the day was already unusually warm for late October and Tran had been edging the borders. Getting a whiff of the heat worked up so far, I complained that he smelled like a goat. Miss Vong turned up her music so loud the sound leaked out of the headphones. Tran's retort was that he would rather smell like an old goat than be one. Miss Vong went for more volume and now her pony tail was bouncing.

Another volley: that if the closest he got to flowers was sitting on a petit-point office chair, he wouldn't smell like a goat either. Then we really had it out—all the grievances and injuries, great and small, banked up over time. I think I even terminated his employment at some point. Finally, he stuffed the Reclining Young Peach in the waste basket (not even a decent burial on the compost) and stalked out.

Later, after I regained a modicum of composure, I found Tran sitting on the bench in the little bamboo grove, chin resting on a spade handle, looking as blue as can be. The grove is his lunchtime retreat, where he lets the dogs finish his usual bowl of pho and often plays a bamboo flute while they nap at his feet. Finally he offered, sotto voce, "I'm sorry." Apologies do not come easily to those of us supremely confident of our opinions. "I'm sorry, too." I had the feeling there was something more he needed to tell me. We sat there for a very long time, first in silence, calmed by the cement Buddha which presides, in a moss-covered state of bliss, over the koi pond, at last giving over to those urges the gardener cannot control: the drive to indulge in flights of fancy about next year.

Q. Dear Miss Mertensia, there is a large congregation of ladybugs outside of our family room window. They have started to find their way into the house, to the consternation of my flamboyant little wife. She has taken to crushing them with the bottom of her sherry glass during particularly intense scenes of *Sorrow's Beacon*. Have I made a mistake in encouraging ladybugs in our garden? They've done a great job in keeping down the aphid population. I sure made a mistake when I phoned home recently during her program; there were nauseating crunching sounds in the background. —*T.C., Birwyck*

A. Dear T.C., Miss Vong and I take our afternoon tea break during the *Sorrow's Beacon* program and we know the very episode—when Doctor Michael told Tamara he was leaving her for his nurse. Miss Vong let fly a barrage of Vietnamese invectives, and I dropped a spoon loaded with lemon curd, which went splattering all over the tray table. It was rough day for the office furnishings.

Oh, just vacuum up the ladybugs and release them outdoors. They're confused by the warm spell we're having and will soon return to hibernation.

Next time ... succulents for winter pleasure

RADICAL PRUNINGS

NOVEMBER 10

Gardening Advice by Mertensia Corydalis

AUTUMN LEAVES

Q. Dear Miss Mertensia, the leaves are falling faster than I can keep up with them, since I am without my partner to help me this year. To tell the truth, I don't care if leaving them lie kills what little lawn is left. Do you think I should take a course to learn how to use a computer? I haven't worked outside the home in years. I am saddened by the prospect of going to an office every day, leaving my beloved garden behind. —*Nelson, Mt. Ashford*

A. Dear Nelson, put on your snappiest sweater (it has to be red) and get outdoors, just a little bit every day if that's all you can manage, and rake up the leaves. The exercise will do you good, clear your head, and let you think things through. It seems as though just about everything revolves around computers these days, so taking a course is a fine idea, and there is the added bonus of meeting new people in your class.

Fortunately the garden chores are winding down, which will give you a few months to catch your breath and establish a new routine. Don't forget to compost. Treat yourself to a leaf shredder if you don't already have one. Miss Mertensia loves you.

Q: Miss Corydalis, thank you for your help with my fern. I followed your advice and repotted it. It recovered nicely and the fronds are thick and green again. Now I have a new problem. My boyfriend Wolfie (he's with Austrian legation in Washington) gave me his bougainvillea to winter over in my townhouse. He had kept the plant on a balcony until it started to get cold at night. When he brought it inside his apartment, he put it by a window near a radiator. It has lost so many leaves, I've basically been given a naked plant to try to save. —*Acqua Tayne, Hamford*

A: Dear Ms. Tayne, I would be put on notice if my boyfriend placed a tropical plant next to a radiator (diplomatic immunity does not extend to disapproval by Miss Mertensia). He may not be good husband material. In any event, give the plant a severe pruning and a good drink and dispatch it to your cool basement so the plant can go dormant. In the spring, after danger of frost has passed, bring the plant outdoors to a sheltered but sunny spot, giving it a good dose of all-purpose houseplant food, and the bougainvillea should soon show signs of renewed growth. You may have noticed, since your last letter was published, that your dance enthusiast Nortie's style of dress has taken a casual turn. My sources over at *Gracious Way* tell me that all his Hermès silk ties were subjected to an untimely demise in the mail-room shredder.

❧❧❧

Q: Dear Miss Corydalis, my name is Ottilie and I am nine years old. The summer I grew big bottle gourds to make into painted birdhouses. I am taking orders now to sell the houses to make money to buy Christmas presents. Do I have to do

anything special to keep them from getting all black and yucky?
—*Ottilie, Mallard Landing*

A: Dear Ottilie; good luck with your enterprise, although I think Mother and Dad, Grandpapa, and Nana would treasure your hand-painted birdhouses more than anything you could possibly buy in a store.

Pick the gourds now that a frost has wilted all the vines. Wipe the gourds with a solution of two tablespoons of household bleach in a quart of water to prevent mold (please ask a grown up for help with this—bleach can just ruin your favorite jeans and T-shirt). Let the gourds dry for about six weeks until you can hear the seeds rattle inside. You will have to speed up the drying by having a small hole made near the neck of the gourd. This will allow the moisture inside to escape. When the gourds are dried, rub off the outer skin with a clean pot scrubber. Get a grownup to help with making holes for the birds to enter, and paint your little heart away. Here at Miltonhurst there is always a bird family in need of a new home, so Miss Mertensia will be contacting you regarding placing an order.

Finally, a motorists' alert: Readers who live in or plan to pass through Hamford should avoid the intersection of Merkle Ave. and Lewis Ct., 21st Street, Rt. 607, and the entire Interstate 70. Miss Vong is enrolled in driving school.

Next time … misting vs. fogging—the great glasshouse debate

WINTER

RADICAL PRUNINGS

DECEMBER 3

Gardening Advice by Mertensia Corydalis

DECKING THE HALLS

Q: Our family tries to be ecologically correct. We're talking about getting a live Christmas tree this year and planting it after the holidays. Any tips? —*Vanya, Cherry Grove*

A: Dear Vanya, most cut trees come from tree farms rather than primeval forests, but if you need a fir tree on your property, then go ahead with the live specimen. There are a couple of problems, the main one being the arid atmosphere inside your house, so you should not have the live tree indoors more than a day or two, which minimizes the decorative value. The other big problem is that conifers should ideally be planted in the spring, giving them a long growing season to get established, so there's some risk involved. Either way, I could never bring myself to buy an artificial tree. The scent of pine evokes the memory of a college summer spent on a hemlock taxonomy project in Quebec, the heady aroma of paper mills, and the amber-eyed Gilles, a barely literate but otherwise diversely skilled conifer-removal technician.

Q. I brought home three small Christmas cactus plants (all the colors were so charming, I couldn't settle on just one). Can I keep them growing and get them to rebloom, or are they just another throwaway seasonal plant? I have kind of a black thumb.
—*Viktor, Petersboro*

A. Dear Viktor, I have bent just about every rule with my huge, nearly twenty-year-old Christmas cactus (*Schlumbergera*), and it faithfully blooms on cue for the holidays, as well as two or three more times during the year. It summers outdoors, hung in an apricot tree where it receives filtered light. I let the plant go nearly dry between waterings. (Rule #1: Do not allow the plant to dry out.) My plant is hung in an east window and receives only a half day of blinding light; thereafter, light whenever someone enters the room and flips the light switch. (Rule #2: Place the plant in medium light and keep in the dark fourteen hours to induce blooming.) My Christmas cactus, now a fountain of bright coral flowers, is very happy in a tiny, toasty breakfast room. (Rule #3: Day temperatures of sixty-five degrees and night temperatures of fifty-five degrees are required for blooming.) If my Christmas cactus were prissy and unforgiving, it wouldn't have lasted longer than certain marriages.

❧❦❧❦

Q. Every year I try to keep my poinsettias going after the holidays. They invariably drop their leaves and never recover. I would like to get them to rebloom.
—*Vronsky, Mokba Station*

A: Dear Vronsky, when it comes to poinsettias I'm afraid I just don't get it. It's not that attractive a plant and it's just not worth the trouble required to keep one going all year, not to mention to do what is needed to make it bloom again. I have seen awestruck crowds in shopping malls admiring twelve-foot-tall pyramids of potted red poinsettias as if they were witnessing Mary in the birthing lounge at Bethlehem General huffing and puffing the Savior into the world. Let me hasten to add, however, that any poinsettia brought to my house as a gift (it's the thought that counts, they say) is appreciated for the splash of color it offers, and I am warming up to some of the delicate pastel shades. If you just have to have a poinsettia put out one big, lavish plant rather than half a dozen dinky supermarket specimens dotted here and there around the house You don't need to decorate every nook and cranny, you know. Poinsettias need plenty of sun to keep growing and most coffee tables don't offer that. The potting medium they are sold in is usually an impenetrable mass, making them difficult to water properly. Feel free to tinker with them.

I believe I have answered all of my neighbor's questions, which arrived in envelopes bearing the Hamford postmark.

Next time ... pucker up: grow a kumquat in your atrium

RADICAL PRUNINGS

DECEMBER 20

Gardening Advice by Mertensia Corydalis

GLAD TIDINGS

Dear Readers,

Miss Vong finally was granted her driving license and she purchased her very own little automobile. That was last week. This week, I received a tearful phone call early in the morning. Miss Vong was going to be late to work because she was going to rot in jail the rest of her life, and could I please bring lots of money to buy her freedom.

Well, to give you the condensed version, at the first police desk I approached, I was told that Miss Vong had become unruly upon being issued a speeding ticket. At the second police desk, I learned that the charges were resisting arrest, being verbally abusive, and assaulting an officer by jumping up and down on his feet with her platform shoes.

A very long while later, after a vile cup of vending machine coffee and a parade of manacled miscreants shuffling by, giving me the curious once-over, I spotted Miss Vong and a very large young policeman chatting and laughing. Officer Steve, as he was introduced by Miss Vong, had dropped the assault charges. He explained that he'd had his safety-toe motorcycle boots on and since she was so tiny and delicate, how much damage could she do, and because her tantrum was in a foreign language, he couldn't be sure whether she had been verbally abusive or not. Officer Steve jotted down Miss Vong's telephone number in his little black book in case further investigation was warranted. So, after paying the fine for speeding, off we went to retrieve Miss Vong's automobile—a not very contrite Miss Vong, I might add, "sprung," as it were, just in time for Christmas.

Q. Dear Miss Mertensia, I am sending you a sage and rosemary wreath, which I learned to make in an herbal crafts class (it was right after the computer class and I wasn't ready to go home yet). It's the season of goodwill and I have some major forgiving to do. It's a tall order, but I think things are going to work out around here. —*Nelson (and Bob), www.wreathsbynelson.com*

A. Dear Nelson, you want to forgive, so you are already halfway there. The wreath arrived in perfectly beautiful and fragrant condition. Allow me to thank you by giving you a little free publicity in my column.

❧❧❧

Q. Dear Miss Corydalis, my mother has given me a puppy for Christmas. My neighbor has a couple of dogs that dug up some rare plant that was a big deal. How can I keep Mr. Pepys from doing things like that in my garden? —*Marley, Hamford*

A. Dear "Marley," Little Benny—excuse me, "Mr. Pepys"— is welcome to come over and play with Jasper and Jennelle any time after Tran has left for the day (his patience is already tested by two dogs). Although rare and valuable plants are hardly a problem in your garden, you can minimize destruction by supervising your puppy outdoors and offering attractive alternatives (such as fetching a tennis ball) to digging up plants. Do not play fetch with sticks until the dog is old enough to discern between a stick and a stake. We're a little old for Mum to be giving us a puppy for Christmas, but "Mr. Pepys" is a happy addition to our neighborhood.

❧❧❧❧

Q. Dear Miss Mertensia, this will be my first Christmas with Hannah, and I feel like I'm home at last. I first saw Hannah, brown as a nut, hair bleached white from the sun, and eyes as big and blue as Delft saucers, working at the nursery. She helped me find a pot of Thai basil and one thing led to another. Hannah is Dutch and she knows all about cooking Indonesian dishes. What would be a great gift for a professional gardener? —*Bettina, North Campus*

A. Dear Bettina, how about a Sheffield steel dibble with a rosewood handle (page 6 in the Mertensia Post Haste Catalogue—monogramming available)? You can't beat a sturdy dibble for planting bulbs! Let me suggest something new to try this summer in your Oriental vegetable garden—Chinese golden melon. Prolific on the vine, the melons are oblong, not much larger than grapefruits, with pale yellow flesh, crisp yet juicy, not unlike honeydew. Imagine a big wooden bowl full of them on the sideboard!

Tran has been busy spending afternoons at the homes of the girls in our Wisteria Study Group, making pine boughs and getting their orchids ship-shape. My daughter Astrid, home from the People's Republic of China, popped in on our club's Christmas tea and decided we needed an Amelia Faye Beauty Products makeover, so we've all been moisturized, contoured, outlined, glossed, buffed, and highlighted for the holidays. Astrid brought home a pair of antique pierced oxblood orchid pots and photos of a deep purple—nearly black—tree peony named the Brooding Young Lover, which Master Chen Xie Lin has been hiding from peony poachers. For the right price, it is mine.

Next time ... get cereus about night blooming

RADICAL PRUNINGS

JANUARY 10

Gardening Advice by Mertensia Corydalis

NEW YEAR'S RESOLUTIONS

Dear Readers,

This morning, Miss Vong dropped a three-pound wedding dress magazine, bristling with yellow sticky notes, on my desk and held out her left hand. The "dreamy" Officer Steve has given her a diamond ring that must have cost him a year's extra duty pay guarding the local toy superstore.

She is on the phone now, plotting a little winter getaway to Florida with Officer Steve. I am deliberating: should Miss Vong wear a *Gone with the Wind* dress that is as wide as she is tall, or should she wear a lovely red silk *ao dai*? It could be a summer garden wedding here at Miltonhurst. The pergola must be covered with New Dawn roses entwined with Comtesse de Bouchard clematis. I shall enlist my expert chef friend (whom you know from the "Ask Yvette" column in *Gracious Way Magazine*) to make a fabulous croquembouche sprinkled with pink nonpareils. There will also be a towering butter cake, all fondant and filigree, the ramparts covered in tiny sugar flowers, a fleet of little pastry barquettes filled with truffled *mousse de jambon*, hand-painted flaky pastry cakes filled with sweet bean paste, some with lotus seed paste, and moon cakes with duck egg yolks inside (I hope Mr. Binh the confectionery manager at the Hanoi Hut Grocery and Carryout has forgiven Miss Vong by now).

Perhaps Madame Bich will come, and she will commandeer my kitchen. I have heard the venerable Madame Bich on the speaker phone, the universal maternal message of guilt beamed by satellite to her two youngest and most difficult children from a world away. But she should be overcome with happiness now, Tran having left for his holiday visit a few days ago, bearing duffel bags full of presents and requests: yard goods, vitamins, over-the-counter remedies, toiletries, toys, and who knows what else.

The household is emptying out at an alarming pace. My daughter Astrid has returned to China to deal with an urgent cosmetic crisis. Counterfeits of the popular Amelia Faye Bedtime Cell Renewal Creme—right down to the celadon green simulated-porcelain jars—are turning up in Guangdong.

Snow is falling. I know this without even looking out the window, because the tires of passing cars are muffled and the birds, which had been chattering at the feeders, have retreated to the hearts of evergreens.

Q. Dear Miss Corydalis, I sold all my gourd birdhouses. My Dad and I went to the garden store to see if they have gourd seeds for sale yet. I can't wait. This year I'm going to grow more kinds of gourds. When I grow up I want to be a garden lady like you. Did you have to go to a special school? —*Ottilie, Mallard Landing*

A. Dear Ottilie, I am admiring the gourd birdhouse I purchased from you. With the painted pink and blue and yellow daisies surrounding its base and trees bearing birdhouses themselves, it will be a garden within a garden outdoors. When the time is right to hang it in the crabapple tree near my kitchen window, I expect there to be some squabbling over who gets to occupy the house.

To answer your question, the oddest thing happens when you proclaim yourself an expert on some topic. People will soon seek out your advice and expect answers. People want answers.

If you wish to learn all the fancy Latin names of plants and their parts, and if you wish to impress enough people with this and other knowledge, so much so that they will pay you for the privilege, you must study horticulture in college. Then they will call you a garden lady.

However, if you wish to be a gardener, as you already are, you will attain higher and higher levels of knowledge and enlightenment with each year of first-hand experience. I have visited thriving plots in the most run-down neighborhoods you can imagine, the gardeners owning not much more than a hoe, a fork, and a spade, planting only seeds saved from year to year, but who still have something to teach another gardener. I have also visited estate-size gardens conceived and maintained by individuals with no formal training, some of them elderly people whose old bodies spring into action the moment they step outdoors. And there are those whose bodies only permit them to think and look and dream, but they are also gardeners. The doers and the believers can know just as much as the heavy thinkers.

SOME CLOSING NOTES:

To television anchorpeople (who purport to have university degrees in "communications") the word for leaves is pronounced *fo-li-age*. "Foil-age," if there is such a word, must have something to do with the sport of fencing or wrapping up leftover food. Resolve to master your native tongue.

And...

All of you who have inquired about the Readers Survey results will be disappointed to learn that, according to Miss Vong, the computer program which contained every morsel of the data mysteriously "crashed" the other day. All was lost and can never be retrieved. We were so close to knowing the answers.

Next time ... get structure in your life, think shrubs

RADICAL PRUNINGS

JANUARY 31

Gardening Advice by Mertensia Corydalis

BLUE CARP

Do I know if it was a philter or a love charm
that caused me to forget the fish down in the pond,
the river where I used to take cool baths, the stars up
in the sky?

Vietnamese folk poem

Dear Readers,

Miss Vong, who is in Florida with her Officer Steve, and Tran, who is on the other side of the world, missed a little excitement around here. When the weather turned bitterly cold, I tried to build a fire in the office-library hearth, and the room was immediately filled with billows of smoke. One of our Hamford Fire Department's finest discovered several bags of unopened letters stuffed, strangely, up the office fireplace flue. A chilly hour of having the French doors flung wide open cleared the air, and no harm was done. As soon as Miss Vong returns from vacation, we will be responding to your questions. First, however, I think an interrogatory or two regarding *les lettres fumées* can be expected.

Snow continues to fall. The first winter Tran and Miss Vong were here, neither had seen snow and neither could stop shivering from the cold, even with their new boots and down jackets. The only way to get over it is to just jump in and wallow, so to set the example, I fell back into a drift and made a snow angel. It took some cajoling, and I caught the rolling of their eyes, but they politely lay down and made their angels on either side of me. There was a little chuckling all around as we brushed snow off each others' backs and stamped our boots on the sidewalk. This will be their fourth winter. They still hate the cold, but I think even Miss Vong would be up for a snowball fight today.

The garden is as new and full of surprises as if it were the first day of June. The iron leaves and vines of my main garden gate have a tracery of snow, and there is a meringue ribbon piped along the top of the iron fence. A statue of Bacchus, always the party boy, wears a pillow on his head. The contorted hazelnut is a fountain of lacy convoluted twigs and deep gold catkin pendants, and nearby, the apricot, its two main branches espaliered into a heart, is an early valentine.

But there are casualties. A Japanese butterfly maple, planted in its own whiskey-tub landscape, the roots trained over thoughtfully chosen stones, has heaved up from the soil. The winter treats in the cold frame—radicchio, some forced witloof endive, rouge d'hiver lettuce, tatsoi—despite the warmth of neighbor rabbit Osmond's contributions and the insulating blanket of snow around the glass, are finished. And the fig, bedded in straw in the garage, is a worry.

There is little to do outdoors but carefully brush the heaviest snow off shrubbery with a broom and keep the bird feeders filled to the brim. I was instructed by Tran, before he left, to maintain an open space at one edge of the lily pond for the koi. There was a hard freeze, and I made excuses for myself about taking a hatchet to the ice. Now, a week later, it has warmed up and the edge of the pond has thawed.

The dogs are having a fine time burrowing their muzzles in the snow and snorting. They chase each other on the surface of the pond, sliding and crashing into the tufts of rush poking through the ice. I chop away at the thin edge of the pond, and the gases of death pour out. The three koi are mounted on the underside of a pane of ice. How beautiful they are: milky-white, with red-gold spots, each different, their gossamer fins and tails fanned out. How they must have suffered, desperate, their gills collapsing.

The dogs come to look at them. I've let so many things perish from neglect. I have not been a good steward of my own garden. When I give them over to the compost bin, I recall that three years before, when they were released into the pond, I had baptized them Athos, Porthos, and Aramis.

It seems that I have no room left for questions in this issue. My apologies.

Next time…the winter potting shed

RADICAL PRUNINGS

FEBRUARY 14

Gardening Advice by Mertensia Corydalis

PHUONG (THE PHOENIX)

The water flows and babbles—
the goldfish fans out its phoenix tail.
Once away from you, I'll still love you.

Vietnamese folk poem

Q: Dear Mertensia, every day a new garden catalogue comes in the mail and now it's time to fill out the order blanks. I'm sitting up in bed, surrounded by catalogues, and I don't know where to begin. I want everything. Please, some advice.
—*Letitia, Bienvue*

A: Dear Letitia, I too am sitting up in bed surrounded by the catalogues, and even though I am a lifelong gardener, I want everything—lately I find myself even desiring hot-colored perennials—and don't know where to begin. My order lists, totted up, come to thousands of dollars, then are crossed off and revised to come to hundreds of dollars. Sometimes I am so caught up in greed and lust over some hard-to-find specimen I can barely breathe. Then the next day, I think I can live without the plant in question but another one takes its place. Start by reviewing what you already have. Then make some sketches of your garden. What is needed to fill the empty places? What will complement the colors and textures you now have? This is one time when you can buy beauty. Don't neglect to consider your obligation to nurture it once you have it in your possession.

My house is like an orchard in spring. As is the custom during Tet, before he left on his trip Tran filled the house with cuttings of apple, plum, and quince branches to be forced into flowering, so I will have good fortune during the coming year. The blossoms are opening, and as I pass from one room into the next I am almost startled by their sweet perfume. Some blossoms already fall in silent flutter, a pink snow on the floor.

Today I went to the potting shed for a fresh saucer of paper whites to force. I have been bringing in pots of bulbs since Christmas, but there still remain rows of paper whites, muscari, freesia, potted up for forcing. The shed is thick with the aroma of bark chips, peat, finely screened compost, humus-rich garden earth, making up all the different potting mixes—for seed starting, for the common houseplants, for terrestrial orchids, for epiphytic orchids, the bins labeled in Tran's big looping hand. Every tool has its place, at the ready like a surgery: pruners, loppers, and saws. Along the walls: rakes, forks, a warren hoe, a poachers spade (so many implements invented to go after rabbits, now put to better use). On shelves: glass cloches arranged in ascending order of size. In the bench drawers: cotton string, hemp twine, raffia, jute cording. In biscuit tins, bundles of labels: short-lived wooden sticks for vegetables, zinc labels mostly for the benefit of unguided and misguided tourists, copper foil tags. In tall baskets: bamboo stakes of different sizes, twiggy branches that show promise as plant supports with a bit of whittling. My own mud shoes, clean as a whistle (when did I last wear them?), on a high shelf. Except for Tran's wellies standing next to the door, these are mostly my things, accumulated over a third of a century, but they have become his things. Landless, he is the gardener.

I changed the page on Tran's new calendar for this year—twelve months of pretty Asian women in swimsuits astride motorbikes—to the month of February. There is reassurance in seeing the year plotted out, square by square, the task in Vietnamese, the name of the plant in English or Latin (often not spelled exactly right, but no matter). A photo fell from behind the calendar. It was of a young woman in a crisp white nurse's uniform such as we no longer see in American hospitals, her calm gaze surely the kindest medicine at her disposal. On her lap, a young child, peacefully bored, a tiny truck in his fist. They are seated in a garden of ginger lilies that exists only in the photographer's backdrop. Under the message on the back, there was the signature "Phuong," a wee heart replacing the tone mark under the "o." I'll say nothing, but nothing will ever be the same. Oh, I know, eventually it will come out. There will be some hot tears, and then he will ask me to sponsor them to join him in this country. And in the end, I will. And if he loves her, then so will I.

Pain passes; the beauty remains.

—*Pierre-August Renoir*

SPRING

She was the ✳ Apple of his Eye

THE SECOND YEAR

RADICAL PRUNINGS

MARCH 13

Gardening Advice by Mertensia Corydalis

ABSINTHE AND MALUS

Dear Readers,

This winter our afternoon tea break with Miss Vong and *Sorrow's Beacon* became a party of three, Officer Steve joining us now on the library divan. It seems that Officer Steve has been a fan for quite some time, watching the program in the coffee shop where he would enjoy his afternoon doughnut. His favorite character is Police Commissioner Reynolds, who personally investigates every jewel theft, poisoning, and transient amnesiac in his jurisdiction.

We had been anticipating today's episode all week. Doctor Michael's car skidded off a lonely rain-slick road. Knocked unconscious and bleeding from a scalp wound, his head rested against the window. At that very moment, Tamara, facing a possible miscarriage after learning that her conniving stepmother had managed to disinherit her, was calling from her hospital bed for Doctor Michael.

Officer Steve looked over the rim of his teacup at Miss Vong and inhaled deeply. "Is that jasmine?" She never took her eyes off the television set. "Unh-unh. Ylang-ylang."

He selected an apple-blossom-shaped cake and seemed to acquire an immediate love for this dainty Asian delicacy.

It was just like Dr. Michael to drive recklessly, leaving Tamara in pain and penniless. Her husband was never there for her when she really needed him.

Our story over for the day, Officer Steve rose to leave, his leather motorcycle and gun holster creaking, eyes glistening. "I would have handed him a citation for a forty-three-oh-two."

Your letters:

Q. Dear Miss Mertensia, I am a fan of Toulouse-Lautrec and am fascinated by absinthe. Is wormwood easy to grow? Can I grow it from seed? If not, where can I buy plants? At what stage will it pack the biggest wallop? Do you have a recipe?
—*Thorpe, East Nova*

A. Dear Thorpe, wormwood is not difficult to grow. In fact, like many artemisias it will spread like wildfire, crowding out anything nearby with no encouragement from you whatsoever. However, we are here to help you with your garden quandaries, not to serve as your mixology consultant. Miss Mertensia is not going to assist you in chasing the Green Faerie by providing recipes for hallucinogens.

Dear Readers,

Recently your Miss Mertensia experienced a bout of insomnia. Rather than doing something useful, e.g., making yet another attempt to actually read *Remembrance of Things Past* or going downstairs to my office and answering your letters, I made the mistake of perusing the cable TV channels. *Great Moments in Ladies' Golf*. No. *The Amazing Electric Self-Stirring Bain Marie* ("Now your family can enjoy creme anglaise every night of the week"). No. Move on. *Pastor Richter's Inspiration Hour* ("Jesus wants you to invest in real estate"). No. What else but GWN (Gracious Way Network)—it's on twenty-four hours a day, seven days a week, as you must know by now. Delphine Doyle (married to my former husband Norton) will show you how to personalize your paper towels, how to strip and refinish a grand piano, how to spit-roast a brace of *poussins*.

This evening Norton is featured in an asparagus-root-planting segment. He explains how to differentiate between male and female asparagus plants (a nuance which occasionally eludes him in his real life). I notice that Norton is now in his Amish phase of garden attire, with a collarless homespun shirt fastened right up to the Adam's apple, blue twill trousers with suspenders, and a broad-brimmed straw hat. I expect to see him hitching up a Percheron to the plow in the next segment.

Later in the program, the camera catches Delphine entering her library (the life unscripted), where Norton is seated before a crackling fire.

"Oh hello, darling," Norton says, looking up from his custom-bound volume. Delphine tells us that she recently had all the wing chairs upholstered in the green, red, and gold tartan of Doyle's tribe as a special anniversary surprise. "So thoughtful of you, darling," says Norton.

Delphine leans over the back of his wing chair and nuzzles his ear. "Oh, Nortie," she says in a newly acquired brogue, "your anniversary largesse was equally impressive.'"

I understand that the late Elvis Presley took a pistol to his television set from time to time. The practice has some merit.

Q. Dear Miss Corydalis, in a nursery catalogue I saw lady apple saplings listed. They are so bright and dear in Christmas decorations pickled as a garnish for a roast turkey, I've decided I must plant a tree. How long will it take for the tree to produce little apples? I've never grown a fruit tree before. Do you have any tips?

—*Chloe, West Trillen*

A. Dear Chloe, first, as with all members of the Malus family, more than one specimen must be planted in your garden to ensure cross-pollination. The other apple trees need not be the same variety, but you must let the nurseryman recommend a suitable pollinator which will bloom at the same time. Look into heirloom varieties— don't waste your efforts on some variety of apple readily available in any supermarket. Consider the placement and ultimate size of the tree very carefully. Miss Mertensia herself underestimated the ambition of her Belle of Georgia tree, only to have it extend branches across a fence and pelt a neighbor's auto with dead-ripe peaches.

Planting a fruit tree is an act of faith that in two or three years—as much as seven for some apples, so much depends on the growing conditions—the tree will eventually bear fruit and that you will own the property for a very long time. The thought of a new owner coming along and cutting down your fruit trees is too painful to contemplate. You can have a tomato growing in a pot on a balcony, or you can have an acre of grass with a little island of bedding plants, but having fruit trees makes a real garden, and a real garden is what makes you a landed person.

꛰꛰꛰

Q. Miss Corydalis, how soon can I begin applying crabgrass control to my lawn? This year, I'd like to get a jump on the problem. —*Donald, Mountebank Heights*

A. Donald, one can hardly hear one's own thoughts over the roar of lawn mowers. The men in my neighborhood seem to have spent a long, restive winter dreaming of the moment when they could get out, give the starter a firm yank, feel the engine explode into action, and trim their turf. We will have to review our no lawn-care questions policy with our secretary Miss Vong. Miss Mertensia does not entertain crabgrass concerns.

Next time… a visit to the Hamford Herbarium algae collection

RADICAL PRUNINGS

APRIL 1

Gardening Advice by Mertensia Corydalis

SO MUCH GROUND TO COVER

Dear Readers,

During these busiest days for the gardener, we find ourselves making daily, sometimes twice-daily, rounds of the nurseries (new stock arrives continually), attending the big garden shows, planning our Open Days, and making plans to visit other gardens around the city, the nation, the world. Someone out there has always come up with some clever idea that never occurred to you and which you may feel free to steal. As always, I urge you to carefully investigate tour operators with whom you are not familiar, which a letter from our reader Nettie will illustrate.

Gardening can be a dirty business.

Q: Dear Mertensia, I am enclosing a brochure from the Global Garden Endowment Fund, an educational organization which guarantees its benefactors lifetime admission to all the public gardens of Europe. Donors at the "Trellis Topper" level also are offered luncheon and a chance to rest and freshen up in the

Benefactor Lounge at each location. The gals and I love to travel and tour gardens, so we are cashing our bonds and writing our checks. Is the director, John L. Corydalis related to you? We're your most ardent fans. We read your column aloud at our garden club meetings. —*Nettie, Waverly Dam*

A. Dear Nettie, I am so pleased that your club enjoys my columns. There is no connection whatsoever between me and this organization. The name is just an odd coincidence, although the director, as pictured in the brochure, does vaguely resemble my brother Artur.

I hope you haven't written those checks yet, because lifetime, or even annual, memberships in all the national horticultural societies of the U.K. and continental Europe would offer you unlimited visits, journal subscriptions, and discounts at the gift shops, and the total would not begin to approach the required donation mentioned in the brochure. I think you should be put on notice about this organization. In addition, Artie has blond hair, what is left of it, and does not wear glasses. No, it's just a coincidence.

❧❧❧❧

Q. Help, Mertensia! My favorite garden store has a huge selection of gladiolus bulbs this year and I would like to plant a variety of shades. However, last year my glads had long, thin strips chewed out of the leaves and most of the flower buds were deformed and never opened. I was so disappointed I didn't even bother to dig them out and save them for this year. What can I do? —*Corintha, West Olive*

A. First of all, dear Corintha, we refer to the "bulbs" as corms. Secondly, the corms probably came to you already infested with the eggs of thrips, a chewing, sucking insect. In our climate the thrips did not overwinter in the rotting corms. For good measure, before you plant new corms, rinse them in a weak solution of water and household bleach. Try a thrips trap, which is a sticky blue tape (thrips love the color blue) fastened to a stake in the gladiolus bed. I hope you are planning to grow your glads in a dense patch for cutting, because they look pretty silly stuck here and there, bobbing and weaving, standing out like a very drunk guest who has turned up at the wrong New Year's Eve party. Also, you may have noticed that glads buds open from the bottom of the stalk upwards, so while they are splendid in hotel-size arrangements, they can be just as useful cut down as the bottom flowers are spent and used in little arrangements with other flowers.

❧❧❧❧

Readers, while we are prowling the display beds at the nurseries, let's not forget an azalea or two to add to our display. Punctuate the varied green textures of a woodland garden with white flowering azaleas. Or carpet a shaded slope with random tufts of red, pink, magenta, orange, violet—Miss Mertensia is giving you permission, on a one-time basis only, to indulge yourself with a spring color tutti-frutti. Which brings us now to an azalea question:

Q. I saw a reference to "cloud pruning" in an article about azaleas. What is this? —*Lester, Bienvue*

A: This is a Japanese technique of pruning a dense shrub like an azalea in multiple levels, somewhat like a fluffy cumulus cloud, as opposed to creating a flat or domed top surface of the shrub. Done well, it is very graceful. However, continuing the subject of plant torture, the concept has evolved into all kinds of wildly expensive nursery stock tormented en masse. While on a recent trip to my favorite nursery, I observed the staff buzzing around a locally famous businessman. This chap, whose talent at marketing auto transmissions has rendered him an expert on virtually every discipline, including fine arts, architecture, sociology, and mass transportation, was shopping for pricey "trophy conifers." Attired in a stiff little gray suit, he delegated tasks to his minions via cell phone, at the same time settling on a collection of junipers clipped into pom-poms. Even my former publisher's Milanese sentry poodles, Funghi and Lucullus, are not trimmed into topiaries!

Note: A trip to the nursery should be done in your gardening togs, so, fired up by the mind-boggling selection of plants, by the camphory smell of cypress mulch, by splashing through the puddles and ducking the nurserymen's watering wands, you can race home and plant your new treasures with no interruption.

Next time… should we leave growing rutabagas up to Canada?

RADICAL PRUNINGS

APRIL 13

Gardening Advice by Mertensia Corydalis

WATCH OUT FOR THAT OLD HORN WORM

Q. Dear Miss M., my very thoughtful husband grows wonderful tomatoes just for me (he gets rashes). My question is about the mothballs he sprinkles among the tomato plants to ward off hornworms and squirrels. I hesitate to question his judgment, but I wonder if this is a safe practice. He's been barricaded in his basement workshop a lot lately, hammering and sawing, something very secretive, so I don't want to interfere when he gets out in the fresh air and gardens.

—*Terramunda, East Hamford*

A. Terramunda dear, There are two formulas for mothballs: naphthalene and paradicholorobenzene. Now does either of those formulas sound like it might go nicely with a fresh tomato-and-kalamata-olive pizza? What exactly is your husband doing in the basement workshop? If I don't hear from you soon I am calling the authorities.

Q. Dear Miss Corydalis, I am attracted to the idea of taking up home winemaking as a hobby. I would like to try something different, unique—like kiwi wine. How are kiwis grown? —*Morris, South Oleander*

A. Dear Morris, first, you must select a hardy variety of kiwi, which should be the only type available at your local nursery. Then you must have at least one male plant as a pollinator and up to three or four female plants in the harem. (So far we have spent about $35.) Since kiwi is a vining plant, you must build a trellis or arbor to support your kiwis (lumber: $100; carpenter: $300). Now you will need a few garden supplies: pruners ($25) and a bag of composted cow manure ($4). In September, when you harvest the kiwis, you will need a fruit press (minimum $100), a basic winemaking kit ($40 and up), bottles (let's say you opt for hand-blown Spanish bottles at $15 each), corks and a corking device ($45). After all this effort, you will want some handsome labels to show off a little (graphic designer: $750). Now you need racks to cellar and age your bottles of kiwi wine (lumber $100; carpenter: $300). Finally, friendship-repairing gifts the Christmas following the one in which you give out your bottles of kiwi wine should be a minimum of $50 each.

Not to stifle your creative urges, but I recommend that you enjoy a good bottle of Beaujolais nouveau (under $20), make a snack of a few kiwis from the supermarket ($1), and peruse a catalogue from a nursery that specializes in wine-grape root-stock (free).

To all my readers, a reminder: if you are planting out annuals (why are you wasting your time on bedding annuals?), remember to tease your roots.

Finally, the mix-up between the Corydalis fellow of the Global Garden Endowment Fund and my brother Artur continues. Or maybe Artie parked his rental car somewhere and forgot to return it. In any event, if any of you readers see a parked silver Mercedes-Benz SL 500 Roadster that doesn't seem to belong to anyone, please call my office. The leasing agency is pestering me to death.

Next time... get tough on thug plants... Siberians: the husky iris

---

FROM OUR CATALOGUE:

CLOCHES, mouth-blown in Czechoslovakia. Large order returned because customer didn't like bubbles in glass. Custom-etched with initials MS. Give your seedlings the edge this spring. Condensation will obscure monogramming. 24", 18", and 12" tall. Call for closeout pricing.

RADICAL PRUNINGS

MAY 1

Gardening Advice by Mertensia Corydalis

CAN YOU DIG IT!

Dear Readers,

Recently, at the end of the day, Miss Vong startled me by pulling a chair up next to my desk. There seemed to be some hesitation, as though she were delaying the announcement of bad news. "Miss Mertensia," she began, "what do you think about checks and bounces?"

Oh no! Now our Miss Vong is in fiscal distress. "It's very expensive to make mistakes with your bank account. But it can happen to anyone," I offered, expecting a request for an advance on her pay.

"Not bank account! Government. Checks and bounces, like the Mr. President, the Madame First Lady, Mr. Speaker of the Congress, and the Supremes. Is it good?"

"Oh, I understand. Balances. Well, the First Lady isn't officially part of the government." So beside myself with discovery of this newly revealed dimension of Miss Vong, I launched into a one-woman debate of the pros and cons. She listened carefully, nodding from time to time. I must have gone on for ten minutes, complete with hypothetical illustrative situations.

Suddenly, she stood up and tossed her long hair with a snap. "Okay thanks," was all she said.

Q. Dear Miss Corydalis, this is a question more about planting than about plants. No matter how sharp I keep the edges of my shovel and how much organic material I add to my soil to keep it loose, just digging a little hole to plant a tomato results in a backache. How do other gardeners do it? —*Byron, Hamford*

A. Dear "Byron," even if I didn't have first-hand knowledge of what the problem is, your letter would tell me you are misusing your implement. As my late father, the renowned landscape architect Perseus Corydalis, taught me from the beginning, "The Right Tool for the Job." The purpose of a shovel is to move material from point A to point B. Spades are for digging holes and edging borders. Forks are for loosening and turning soil, as well as for digging up and dividing perennials. A proper fork would solve your problems. Now that your backaches will soon disappear, your mother won't have to drive all the way from her retirement community to continue excavating that fishpond you have been working on for a year.

Your little Benny (a.k.a. "Mr. Pepys")—now there's an efficient digger. I can start to see a glimpse of Kowloon Harbor through that hole he has made under my fence in his futile campaign to seduce my Jennelle. We would appreciate your replacing the dirt and issuing a stern reprimand.

Q. Dear Miss Mertensia, is there going to be a garden contest again this year? The yellow rubber garden shoes I won last year are too sharp to wear in the garden. I like to put them on when I go out special. My friends at Rhonda's Basshole Cafe and Bait say, "Buddy, you never go fishing with us no more." I tell them, "Fellows, I'm into this garden thing. I've caught the Mertensia Fever."

I would like to meet you and see your garden. I figure it's only a four-hour drive from Rising Creek to Hamford. I have a whole lot of garden questions. I could take you out to supper. You wouldn't have to put me up or nothing. I will stay at a motel. Just say the word.

—*Buddy, Rising Creek*

A. Dear Buddy, I couldn't bear to be responsible if your garden suffered from neglect while you traveled to Hamford just to meet me. I will be happy to answer any of your garden questions by mail. If a book store ever opens in Rising Creek, you may be assured that my publisher will send me there to autograph copies of my books.

This is the perfect time to announce this year's contest: the theme of the garden is to be a Fred Astaire and Ginger Rogers Reverie. While ornamental objects are a plus, the focus is on the selection of plant material. You must send photographs and a plant list. Prizes will include a year's subscription to *Radical Prunings* and selections from the Mertensia Post Haste Catalogue of Garden Accessories. And yes, last year's winners are eligible to enter and win again.

Closing Notes: My brother Artur would appreciate a few pen pals, especially ladies, as he is temporarily inconvenienced. I can deliver your letters when I visit him, as soon as my busy schedule permits. One of life's little lessons: never forget to turn in your rental car when you are through with it.

Next time... how to keep your spinach from bolting

RADICAL PRUNINGS

MAY 15

Gardening Advice by Mertensia Corydalis

SPECIAL SUMMER CLEARANCE ISSUE

We have solved the mystery of Miss Vong's sudden interest in civics. Again she approached me at the end of the day. "How come the national song is not 'America the Beautiful' instead of that other song?" she asked. "It's all about bombs and rockets. It's hard to sing, too."

"Because," I explained, "given a choice, before sports events most Americans prefer violence over poetry."

"OK. What is the Vice President's job?"

"To wait for the unthinkable to happen," I answered.

"Hey, that's not the answer! He presides the Senate."

In spite of that, I passed the tutor test, and it was agreed that I would help her study for the citizenship exam.

Now, from our Mertensia Post Haste Catalogue of Garden Accessories, some selections only for my readers:

MAJOLICA SLUG TRAP. Hand-painted slug and hosta motif. Beer not included. Reg. $39.95. Sale $29.00.

Protect your precious perennials. **GRYPHON HOSE FENDERS.** Order plenty! Reg. $10.99 each. Sale $6.99 each.

CALLIGRAPHY-ENGRAVED SOLID COPPER PLANT MARKERS. Weather to a lovely verdigris. Send plant list. Sorry, Latin names only. Reg. $18.00 each. Sale $15.00 each.

Exclusive to our catalog. **CHANTERELLE MUSHROOM COMPOST.** Pamper your favorites. One-cubic-foot bags. Reg. $9.99 each. Sale $8.00 each (Add $1.50 per bag additional shipping.) Portobello Mushroom Compost Sold Out.

STERLING POTTING-SOIL SCOOP. Start your holiday shopping early. These will go fast! Reg. $175.00. Sale $ 159.00. Add $15.00 for monogramming.

To order, visit us online at
Mertensia Post Haste and don't forget
to add your name to our mailing list
to receive our big Fall Catalogue!

And finally, her studies have caused Miss Vong to allow this letter to cross my desk:

Q: I just wanted to let your readers know that a small number of dandelions in the lawn can be easily controlled by a hollow plastic cane which dispenses herbicide when poked into the center of the weed. —*Kandy, West Jefferson*

A: I suppose I am expected to grudgingly applaud your judicious use of chemicals, which set me to thinking how my mother, a thrifty French housewife, dealt with dandelions. She dug up the very young tender leaves with a paring knife, steamed them, and dressed them with butter, olive oil, and lemon. (Believe me, as soon as you begin viewing a wild plant as a delicacy, it will make itself scarce.) A philosopher once wrote that we fail to value poor children, because, like dandelions, there are so many of them. But children readily recognize the simple beauty of the blossom. After all, as a toddler was not a dandelion bloom the first object of nature you deemed beautiful and valuable enough to present as a gift to the person you loved most in the world, your mother? And did your mother not put the blossom in a glass of water and set it where she could admire it while she washed dishes? I fear that suburban children whose yards are subject to Four-Step chemical programs will never hold a dandelion flower—let alone a buttercup—under each other's chins to see the intense yellow reflection which signifies that one loves butter. (Who doesn't love butter?) Nor will then puff on the ethereal seed head, startling the cat and sending the little tufts of silk off on their mission.

Readers, I'm having Miss Vong separate your letters into two piles: one for real gardening questions and one for lawn-care questions. I shall read your lawn-care letters after I retire from my career as an astronaut.

Next time ... pricking out seedlings ... sowbug control

BAG
WORM

SUMMER

RADICAL PRUNINGS

JUNE 4

Gardening Advice by Mertensia Corydalis

POSTCARD FROM THE SMOKY PLATFORM

Dear Readers,

Recently we opened our own Miltonhurst to the public as part of the Twilight Garden Tour to benefit the Hamford Center for Disruptive Children. It is always entertaining to meet and chat with our readers. So many of you ladies had questions for Tran that he was a little swamped. Please write if he was unable to address your problems.

We would like to respond to a review of the tour which appeared in the *Hamford Cornet*. The guest columnist Norton Doyle, who seemed to admire these gardens when they were still tended by my famous (and well-connected) father, described my perennial beds as "nearly charming in their homespun fecklessness, blowsy with a studied unkempt effect." He was referring to the edging of alyssum encouraged to spill over and soften the edges of the pea-gravel footpaths and phlox planted near the front of the borders so their flower heads bow and nod at the passerby. He goes on, "One can almost visualize the tender Hansel and Gretel, disoriented by the vegetative profusion, stumbling down the pea-gravel paths toward the main house and their Destiny." The criticism comes from a typewriter gardener who views Nature as an unruly employee always in need of close supervision and correction. Some of us actually leave our air-conditioned offices and get our knees dirty out of doors.

Q. Dear Miss Mertensia, I know you were real surprised when I just showed up at your doorstep, but you were real nice to show me around your garden. It's the most beautiful garden anyone could imagine. You're not too bad yourself, neither. No wonder you need that Oriental fellow to help you out. It's too much for one lady to keep up. Also thank you for answering all my garden questions at supper. I hope I didn't embarrass you or nothing. You will be happy to know that my garden was just fine when I got home. My cousin's kid watered everything just the way I told him. My tomatoes are coming along great this year. Thanks again. —*Buddy, Rising Creek*

A. Dear Buddy, It was a pleasure to meet you. Thank you again for dinner. I cannot recall the last time I enjoyed Salisbury steak and a beer. And the souvenir paperweight from the restaurant gift shop is already put to good use in my office. I am mailing you a copy of one of my books, *The Small Potager* (pronounced po-tah-zhay—it's French for vegetable garden). Keep your tomatoes evenly watered this dry summer to prevent cracking and blossom-end rot.

Dear Readers,

Now that my brother Artur has been sufficiently punished for his memory lapse regarding a certain rental car, I have been getting morose postcards from him, written in the wine bars and cafes of all the botanical gardens of Europe. The confusion between Artie and the director of the Global Garden Endowment Fund resulted in five years probation and restitution, which involves paying for and accompanying Nettie and her friends in the Waverly Dam Garden Club on a whirlwind tour, paying for their horticultural society lifetime memberships and luncheon at each garden. On the bright side, I have been getting postcards from Nettie saying how lovely the gardens are this time of year and how she and "the gals" find my brother Artie charming and amusing. Lady judges seem to see it that way, too. Artie has had more suspended sentences than a beatnik poetry reading.

Here, we have a bumper crop of scallions, so I believe I will try my hand at making a batch of Chinese onion cakes. When my daughter was ten years old, the three of us, my husband Norton, Astrid, and I crisscrossed Sichuan province all summer visiting farms and kitchen gardens for my book on cultivating Chinese vegetables. At just about every farm, the grandmother of the house sent us off with a packet of freshly made scallion cakes: dense, yet flaky, perfumed with sesame oil. Astrid and I were mad for them.

Our train was speeding through Shandong province toward the city of Yantai, where there was an agricultural exposition and a few days of relief from the heat by the sea. Norton asked Astrid to go outside our compartment and watch out the window on the other side of the train. Then I learned that he believed he was meant to do better things with his life than write about vegetables. Meanwhile, Astrid explored the train unattended, until returned by the conductor. She had a game of tiddlywinks with a boy in the soft-seat car who had an extra little thumb growing out of the one on his right hand and then stopped to ask a lot of nosy questions of a trio of People's Army soldiers who were using their furlough for their first visit to the ocean.

The train streaked past fields of cabbages and factory smokestacks and peasants atop the mouths of tunnels using long poles to knock lumps off the heaped coal cars. Norton had already spoken with his editor on the telephone about another project. In the hard-seat car, Astrid played with a well-groomed goat which was also traveling with a family to the agricultural exposition in Yantai. Farmers looked up from their melons growing in long banks of manure and hot compost to wave at us.

Of course, the next year Norton came out with that big coffee table book of society matrons' gardens, assuring him the kind of future he desired. The train whistle screamed as we sped past bicyclists waiting impatiently at road crossings. Before she was finally returned to our compartment, Astrid ordered up, in Mandarin, a crème de menthe ice cream sundae in the dining car.

I chose to see my project through to the end. Norton went on to Beijing to fly back to America. Standing with Astrid on the smoky platform, surrounded by camera equipment, a portable typewriter, and the family baggage, I resolved to never again feel as frightened and alone as I did watching Norton's train get smaller and smaller.

Next time…why we must weed

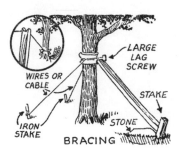

RADICAL PRUNINGS

JULY 17

Gardening Advice by Mertensia Corydalis

WISHING CAN MAKE IT SO

Dear Readers,

Miss Vong, leaving nothing to chance in preparing for her naturalization exam, has memorized the Bill of Rights this week. Of course, we're all humbled, but we probably don't have a Statue of Liberty paper doll taped to our monitors to inspire us.

Q. Ol' Betsy, as I call my lawnmower, is on her last piston. When I go shopping for a replacement, should I get a mulching mower or continue to bag the clippings? —*Mel, Hillcrest*

A. I find it peculiar that a grown man, and a homeowner at that, should be on a first-name level of intimacy with a piece of power equipment. Perhaps this carries over to your recreational activities as well. If you must mow, make it a mulching machine and keep your chemically treated clippings out of the public compost heap. Sorry I can't muster up much sympathy about the demise of your machine.

EXCITING NEW CATALOGUE ITEMS:

BEE SKEPS—Hand-woven by artisan Florence Caudill. Brought to our attention by our very own Buddy of Rising Creek. Fashioned of rushes gathered in "the wet spot over by Rhonda's trailer." Grace your herb garden. Only $40.00 (half of which goes to Mrs. Caudill).

PERUVIAN "PILLS"—Dehydrated and bagged in five-pound packages. A trowelfull of our odorless Andean alpaca "Pills" will get your compost cooking. Only $10.99.

RUSTLED ROSE PRUNERS—Rusty pruners, found on abandoned Texas farms by rose rustlers. Long-lost, for decorative use only. Perfect for the well-appointed potting shed. Now only $24.99 each. Let us select for you.

Next time… grist for the mill: collecting mill stones

RADICAL PRUNINGS

AUGUST 10

Gardening Advice by Mertensia Corydalis

THE PERILS OF FRANCINE

Q. Dear Miss Mertensia, my neighborhood garden center has ornamental grasses on sale. There's a wonderful selection left, and with the prices so low, I could devote a whole new bed to different heights and textures. I've never planted grasses this late in the year. Do you have any tips? —*Armando, Foxdale*

A. Dear Armando, in theory, most perennials can be planted at any time the ground is not frozen. In practice, a new transplant needs time to recover from the shock of being torn from its cozy nursery pot and to establish itself as a new resident of the garden. My friends in the nursery business will never forgive me for this, but even if these plants have been given professional attention all summer, they still have been under a great deal of stress from the extremely hot, dry weather. Moreover, the grasses are beginning to die back as preparation for their period of dormancy. This is not a good year to take advantage of late-season sales. And that's at a real nursery.

Plants at the so-called "garden centers" under the side

porticos of discount department stores have been in the care of adolescents who have to be repeatedly told to pick up their own socks at home. Think about it.

Monday morning came and Miss Vong was late. Very, very late. I thought perhaps she was exhausted after a long evening with her American history textbook, but Tran assured me she had only frosted her bangs and retired early. I telephoned the apartment throughout the day. Worry got the best of me and I hopped into the Buick Roadmaster to find out firsthand what was going on. I found her little car parked behind the apartment building, the driver's door open. The seat belt alarm was chiming, and coins were spilled over the carpet as though Miss Vong and her purse had been wrenched from the car. A zebra-print scrunchie, one of those elasticized ponytail holders, had been blown under a nearby bush. I was nearly faint with fear. Tran had given me a key to the apartment, which seemed to be in order, except no Miss Vong. I was too upset to even take a few minutes to snoop around. There was no doubt in my mind: Miss Vong was missing and not by choice.

We have been writing this column by hand from a hospital bed. We are about to have a little joint surgery, necessitated by the wear and tear of being on our knees in the garden over the years. The preoperative sedative is taking effect, and we will have to tell you the rest about Miss Vong later. Your Miss Mertensia hasn't felt this relaxed since helping to harvest the student horticulture project in the back of one of the university greenhouses.

Next time… magnesium: mineral for the millennium

RADICAL PRUNINGS

SEPTEMBER 14

Gardening Advice by Mertensia Corydalis

FIT TO BE TIED

Dear Readers,

It's been a madhouse here at Miltonhurst. Your gardening queries have been piling up, and if any of you received replies which seemed a little, well, startling, bear in mind that Miss Vong is not a garden professional. When I returned from my convalescence, I discovered a growth of chin whiskers protruding from Tran's face, flawless as a silken crème caramel. With his hair tied back at the nape of his neck, he looked like a mandarin and I was having none of that. I told him to march right upstairs, find a razor, and begone with the chin whiskers. There were sounds of water running and drawers being yanked open and slammed closed. In a few minutes he came bounding down the stairs like a teenager hoping that the new nose ring will go undetected. The whiskers were intact. "Screw you!" he called back as the kitchen door slammed behind him. A few days later the whiskers were gone, but I pretended not to notice.

I promised to continue explaining what happened to Miss Vong, prior to my knee surgery, so here is the rest of the story:

If the Hamford Police Department investigated Miss Vong's disappearance with the same zeal that it pursues every one of her little illegal left turns and parking meter lapses, perhaps your letters would not have gone unanswered for days. Even Officer Steve only reluctantly returned from an out-of-town bowling tournament to assist the Missing Persons Bureau.

Tran and I exhausted every possibility, interviewing all of Miss Vong's girlfriends and ex-boyfriends, including even Mr. Binh, confectionary manager at the Hanoi Hut Grocery and Carry-out, who has bravely endured a broken heart and still provides Miss Vong with delicacies. Several residents of the apartment building where she and Tran live recalled a mysterious black car with deeply tinted windows that had been lurking just down the street. There was no question: Miss Vong had been kidnapped.

A few days later I found an envelope slipped under my front door. Inside was a note composed of cut-out and pasted printed letters: iF you WaNt TO sEE MIss VONG AgaIN BRING $20oOo IN cAsh. I was to bring the money in a briefcase to the St. Francis Hotel Grille at 3 p.m. the next day and leave it under the seat of the booth nearest the door. I recognized the typefaces on the note from GQ magazine and Vogue Hommes.

I sat in the booth nearest the street entrance and slipped the brief case under the seat. There were only three other patrons in the grille: an attractive young couple, business types, obviously carrying on an afternoon affair, and a tall man, wearing a perfectly starched white Egyptian cotton shirt and cream felt borsalino hat pulled down over his face, hunched over his drink at the far end of the bar.

I marched right over to the tall man and spun his barstool around. "Damn you, Artie! What have you done with my secretary?" I demanded.

"Jesus, Tennie, you were supposed to just leave the case and go," he whispered. The bartender looked up from the glasses he was polishing.

"The case is under the booth seat. I want to see Miss Vong right now, Artie, or I'm calling the police."

He dropped a room key into my hand. "The girl eats like a horse! Every time I turn my back she's ordering up room service. I've used up the last of my cash on tips."

Turning the key in the lock, I braced myself for a tearful reunion, Miss Vong flinging her arms around my neck and sobbing uncontrollably upon her liberation. "Miss Mertensia!" she said, glancing away from the television. Miss Vong sat propped up on one of the beds, surrounded by soda cans, bakery-shop boxes of tea cookies, a half-nibbled muffin on hotel china, and a Godiva truffle assortment (several of the chocolates bearing the marks of core sampling). Nowhere in sight were ropes, torn-up sheets, handcuffs; definitely not a gag or any other abduction paraphernalia. She patted the bed next to herself. "Come on, *Sorrow's Beacon* is just starting." Well, this was the episode where we were going to find out once and for all whether Philip is really gay or just pretending so Marcella will break off their engagement, so I joined her on the bed.

I knew it would only take a few minutes for Artie to turn up. He opened the case and flung newspapers and wadded-up plastic grocery bags, the ones you have about a hundred a week to recycle, all over the room. "What is this? Of all the lowest things! Now what am I supposed to do?"

"Artie," I said, "If you think I'm going to cash in a CD just to save your sorry derrière, you are very much mistaken."

"But I had to go buy her a toothbrush and makeup and look at this" —he darted into the bathroom—"special complexion soap. And pajamas. Oh, and the first pair was too big and her bad luck color. So I had to go shopping in the junior miss department at Fielding's for pajamas. Do you know how embarrassing that was? I'm too old to be dating a junior miss and too young to be the father of one!"

Frankly, I wouldn't put either scenario beyond Artur. "Well, Artie, the next time you kidnap someone, you'll just have to give a little notice so the victim can pack an overnight bag."

During the drive home Miss Vong, who was quite happy with her two hundred dollars' worth of new Amelia Faye cosmetics, and I had a little discussion about whether it counts as paid personal days off from work when one has been kidnapped.

Next time…take umbrage: new bulbs for the shade garden

RADICAL PRUNINGS

SEPTEMBER 25

Gardening Advice by Mertensia Corydalis

WE HAVE WINNERS!

Q: Dear Miss Mertensia, while you were convalescing I wrote in with a question about planting fall mums in the ground. I found ones with a gorgeous plum color and would like to winter them over. The reply is signed by your associate, and I'm afraid I'm unclear about her directions. Here is what she wrote:

> "Dear Mr. Bradley, I ask brother Tran how to plant your Mom. He say take pot away from your Mom and make her roots feel crazy. Stick rotten cowshit in your hole. Add special dirt from the garbage pile behind your garage. Push your Mom in the hole and cover tight with dirt. Hose yourself good. Your prostrated servant, Miss Francine Vong" —*Bradley, Surrey Hills*

A: Well, as they say, dear Bradley, "Mum's the word."

It is time to announce the winners of this year's Readers Garden Contest. The theme was a Fred Astaire and Ginger Rogers Reverie, and I was overwhelmed by the creativity of the entries. It was very difficult to select the top three winners, but here they are:

THIRD PLACE goes to Mr. and Mrs. Rose of Midville, a photographer and artist respectively. Their entry is a salute to *Top Hat,* and features a stand of the darkest hollyhock *Alcea rosea* "Nigra," whose blossoms evoke the deep sheen of a tuxedo. In the forefront is a froth of Queen Anne's lace, baby's breath, and the palest pink shaggy English rose Eglantyne. The effect is that of the hem of Miss Rogers' ball gown flashing by as she is swirled off her feet by Mr. Astaire. Bravo! To Mr. and Mrs. Rose we are awarding the Ardent Gardener collection of fragrant perennials from our Mertensia Post Haste Catalogue of Garden Accessories.

SECOND PLACE goes to Lois of Dudley, also a photographer (readers, quality photos of your efforts pay off). The elegant simplicity of her planting is what caught my fancy. The bed is on the rim of a small elevation and consists of a mass planting of coreopsis "Moonbeam" with a thick planting of green Irish moss at its feet. The hundreds of tiny pale yellow blossoms atop the ridge suggest, as Lois writes, "Fred and Ginger at the railing of an ocean liner, looking out at the stars twinkling in the sky and sparkling on the waves." Well done! We have selected our fabulous straw garden-party hat with the largest and most wanton silk roses imaginable as Lois's prize.

Now for **FIRST PLACE**. May I have a drum roll, please. A winner last year, our friend Buddy of Rising Creek has shown an element of design that none other quite achieved: rhythm. Buddy's inspiration was "Flying Down to Rio," and his entry is a bed of undulating swath of the hottest-colored dwarf cannas (I hate this plant, as my readers know, but it's perfect in this situation), sizzling red crocosmias, the POW! of red and yellow hot pokers (Kniphofia), and vibrating ultraviolet heliotrope. I can almost hear the maracas and conga drums. Buddy writes that when the contest was announced he had no idea who Fred Astaire and Ginger Rogers were. Rhonda of Rhonda's Basshole Cafe and Bait helped him select some movies from the video rental section of her bait store and he has become a passionate fan. In fact, he has become so inspired (I assume "inspired" can be a synonym for "turned on," as Buddy puts it) he has been driving to Watley City to take ballroom dancing lessons. He writes that just working in his theme bed makes him want to put on his rumba pants (I can only imagine) and hop in the truck. I am sorry to inform Buddy that Miss Mertensia is recuperating from knee repair and must decline his suggestion that he drive to Hamford and take me club hopping. I am afraid there are no longer supper clubs in Hamford.

For First Prize, we are awarding Buddy our best cedar compost bin, the Executive model (some assembly required). Compost in good health, Buddy, and keep those toes tapping.

Next time… boring beans—are you a legume reactionary?

AUTUMN

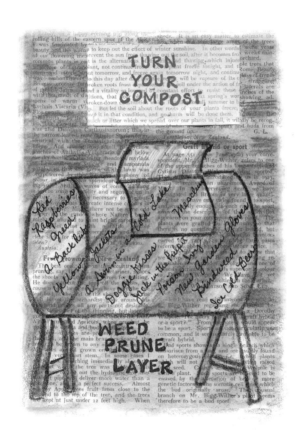

RADICAL PRUNINGS

Gardening Advice by Mertensia Corydalis

ZEN AND THE ART OF BOILER MAINTENANCE

Dear Readers,

Gardening is in the Corydalis blood, probably from the time the first hominid of our clan stood upright just long enough to notice some wildflower that would look better in another location, somewhere a little closer to the family cave. Our avaricious collecting of books on gardening began with Grandfather Corydalis and has continued with my own out-of-control charge accounts with several booksellers. But years of referring to the volumes that line the walls and fill the negative space under nearly every piece of furniture in my office/library (and just about every other room in the house, not even counting cookbooks in the kitchen) and jamming the volumes back into the first accommodating interstice, not to mention the disruption caused by various housekeepers who were only trying to do their job, have resulted in several thousands of books in desperate need of cataloguing and organization. A week-long search for the first edition of my own book *Designing with Hellebores* finally brought me to take action. I am hiring a rare-book librarian from Hamford University to come to my home on his day off each week and make sense of all this chaos.

On to our readers' dilemmas, the first of which is also a problem with too much of a good thing.

Q. Dear Miss Mertensia, this spring, my partner Nelson, who is the gardener in the household, assigned me a tiny out-of-the-way plot (where presumably I won't ruin the aesthetics of "his" garden). I planted a horseradish root, my favorite condiment, and it took over the whole plot, spreading into the rest of the vegetables' territory. I've been told to "use it or toss it." How do I harvest the horseradish and turn it into something edible? —*Bob, Mt. Ashford*

A. Dear Bob, fresh horseradish has a bright flavor that is lost in the bottled grocery store product. Now that the plant is going dormant, you may dig up the roots—and I mean dig. They can be as long as parsnips grown competitively in the U.K. Scrub and peel the roots. I suggest that you set up your grating operation outdoors. Trust me on this. Cut the roots into one-inch chunks and finely chop in your blender or food processor, adding white vinegar to reach the desired consistency. Then you may bottle what you can use within a few weeks. Freeze the rest in small containers. Be sure to seal and wipe off your containers carefully or you will have horseradish-scented ice cream. You have planted an aggressive perennial. Be prepared to never hear the end of it.

When my brother Artur and I were children, our father made

a rare foray into Maman's kitchen. Having grown horseradish as an experiment, he bought a shiny chrome combination juicer and vegetable-processing machine, the cost of which, as well as the space it occupied in the *garde manger*, brought on the formation of storm clouds. Fascinated by the chrome machine, Artie and I watched Father grate fresh horseradish and suffer a torrent of French (this was the occasion when we, or at least I, completed our vocabulary of naughty words in French). A dirty yellow fog reaching with thin, gnarled fingers into the least crevice of the house (but perhaps that is the imagination of a child who overheard Grandfather speaking of mustard gas in the Great War), the fumes were so pungent that Artie and I were driven weeping from the interesting once-in-a-lifetime argument between our parents. This was even more interesting than the Christmas morning when Artie and I burst into our parent's bedroom and discovered Maman entertaining Père Noel. Artie, although three years younger than I, was a little more advanced and explained certain things to me.

Announcing that she had had enough, Maman marched upstairs and packed a huge suitcase. Artie and I watched Maman lug the suitcase down to the street and get in a taxicab. Then the sadness of it all settled on us and we held each other's hand. Abandoned children's tears mixed with horseradish tears.

A little while later, the taxicab returned and Maman dragged the suitcase back up to the front door. We clung to her coat as she swept into the house and announced that it had been a very long time since she had made *boeuf en daube*, with a little horseradish on the side, *pour les enfants*. Us. "Bully beef," observed Father, now stocking the refrigerator with jelly jars of the horseradish. "Bully."

Keep your eye on this invasive perennial. The roots go deep, and it can take over your life if you let it.

❧❧❧

Q: Dear Miss Corydalis, my company transferred me into Zone 5 from southern California this past spring, so I am relearning everything I thought I knew about gardening. Someone told me I can winter over my potted geraniums by washing off all the soil and hanging them upside down from the ceiling in the basement. I'm skeptical. Does this work? —*Nestor, Buchanan Heights*

A: Dear Nestor, first, we are talking about pelargonium, not the hardy perennial geranium, which is an entirely different plant. You don't want dying plants hanging from your basement ceiling. Instead, take cuttings of nonflowering stems about four inches in length from the terminal bud. Remove all but a pair of leaves at the top, dip the stems in rooting hormone, and arrange in moist vermiculite. The cuttings should be rooted in about three weeks, at which time you can pot up the new plants and grow on in a sunny window or under growlights. Discard the mother plant after frost—it is now quite woody and will not make a nice houseplant. I hope the reason you want to keep this plant is some especially nice color or form. I do not much like pelargonia.

In the early, lean years of my postacademic career, I took the position of managing a greenhouse with about fifty thousand red (no other color, just fire-engine red) geraniums being cultivated for the Mother's Day trade. Imagine twelve-hour days facing nothing but the concerns of fifty thousand potted red geraniums. Imagine being subject to emergency summonses seven days a week, no matter whether you were sleeping, sinning, or repenting for the sinning. And, owing to the nightly faltering of the ancient boiler heating system, ventilation by fans wired in an exciting and fanciful manner and clerestory vents opened and closed by banging a hammer, one by one, on warped rods and rusty levers; and the predictable herbal impairment of the plant engineer, the summonses did come seven days a week, and your Miss Mertensia became quite adept at boiler maintenance. As Miss Vong would put it, "I am hating this forever in the time of my life." So much for geraniums.

Today Miss Vong took a telephone call from her mother, barraging Madame Bich with questions in Vietnamese. When the call ended, Miss Vong was all smiles and flushed with excitement. "I have to go talk to Tran," she said and made one of her rare excursions into the garden. When she returned, she said nothing, but her face was no longer bright with joy.

I found Tran in the little bamboo grove where he likes to eat his lunch and collect his thoughts. Actually, the bamboo grove is not so little anymore. He is letting it get out of control and, at this rate, in a few years I'll be in the timber business. He quickly dabbed his eyes with a handkerchief. We talked about the situation, whether he wanted to make a trip to Vietnam as he did at the end of January of this year. He said he needs to work at the Metro Botanical Conservatory for the winter. He needs more money now to send home. Tears welled up in his eyes again and he embraced me, "Miss Mertensia, I am so alone."

Earlier, after the phone call from Madame Bich, I looked up a new word in my Vietnamese dictionary: *em bé*. It means baby.

Next time…hybridizing hemerocallis: plan for a vigorous breeding program

RADICAL PRUNINGS

Gardening Advice by Mertensia Corydalis

THE USUAL SUSPECT

Dear Readers,

Just when I thought I'd seen and heard it all, the meaness of human nature seems to plumb new depths. On a recent crisp fall morning, Tran came to me in a fury. A forest, which had been part of Miltonhurst since Father transplanted our family (not including Artie, who was born the year after we arrived) from the U.K. to Hamford, had vanished. No, this was not a case of Birnam Wood hiking up its kilt and marching off to Dunsinane. This was the work of a cowardly burglar making off with a defenseless, if wildly valuable, penjing miniature willow grove. All that remained was a tiny mud figure, broken on the terrace. The little fisherman had sat patiently by a white marble stream for over a century.

The penjing willows, as well as a gnarled dwarf Chinese elm, were gifts to my grandfather from a master practitioner who had trained these trees all his adult life. As a child, I loved these dollhouse-size landscapes, and although I was not allowed to touch even the least pebble or coin-size patch of spongy moss (obviously I did touch them), I spent hours making up stories about the fisherman in the willow grove and the scholar who sat under the elm writing a book that would never be finished.

Readers report to me all the time the depressing discovery of a very nice potted plant being heisted from their front veranda in the dead of night, and I have been very sympathetic. But it's different when it happens to oneself. I immediately put out the word among members of the serious collecting community to be on the alert for my penjing. One member was, at that very moment, probably writing out a sizeable check.

A report was filed and met with amusement by the Hamford police officers who failed to understand that the theft was greater than most amateur bank robberies. My insurance company took the matter somewhat more seriously, although the situation did not quite fit any of their computer codes, which nearly negates the reality of the loss in their scheme of things.

Barely ten days had passed since the theft when Jasper and Jennelle created a commotion late one night. No matter how careful one is, there is no preventing that massive iron garden gate from squeaking. From my bedroom window I caught a glimpse of a figure in black clothes, switching a flashlight on and off as he made his way through the garden to the lath house where the little scholar under the elm and two Japanese bonsai trees are kept. The thief had come back for the scholar's elm. I pulled on a robe, grabbed my old field hockey stick from boarding school days and went into the garden, the dogs noisily locating the culprit immediately. Just as I was about to confront the thief, another figure dropped out of the nearby peach tree.

"Hai yi!" It was Tran, armed with a spare hoe handle, which he held in both hands like a quarterstaff. The thief groped and found a four-foot-long steel delphinium stake that had been overlooked in the fall cleanup, and he took the en garde position with his improvised rapier.

"Have at it, old boy," the thief challenged.

"Have at your ass, Mr. Artur!" growled Tran.

With the dogs yapping hysterically and me pleading for them to stop, Artie lunged and parried. Tran blocked the delph stake with the ash handle and employed a few swirling leaps that I'm not sure were entirely necessary. Both panting, the two stumbled over the limestone flower bed edgings and crashed into a birdbath. It was a fine example of art pottery, too. I'm just sick about it.

Tran leaped out of the way of a lunge by Artie and was perched, for a moment, on a low stone wall, until he fell flat on his back. Artie thrust the stake at Tran's chest, "Touché!" but the blunted tip would not penetrate a sweatshirt. Tran scrambled to his feet and two resumed swatting and prodding at each other. I think not many blows hit the mark. They were momentarily consumed by a huge oakleaf hydrangea bush, and finally lost their footing and fell into the pond with a tremendous splash. Covered with slime and rotting water lily leaves, the two numbly tried to continue their struggle.

Suddenly Artie clutched at his chest with both hands and collapsed. Tran and I pulled him out of the pond and laid him out on the pavers. He was in crushing pain and was struggling for breath. Luckily the neighbor, who had finally decided to investigate all the shouting and barking, saw what was happening and ran to summon the emergency squad while Tran and I attempted to resuscitate Artie.

I don't know how Artie came to be pilfering and fencing valuable plants, or holding Miss Vong for ransom, for that matter. What happened to the days when Artie could live for a month off a back-of-the-casino poker game and a big, persuasive smile? When a flashy high dive at some resort pool bought him a year's worth of living like a prince? There is no retirement plan for aging confidence men. The Easy Way was always Artie's Way, whether it was me executing his prizewinning science projects at school or some plain little college girl at Wharton writing his macroeconomics term paper for him while he was off chasing a department-store model or a drama student, always the beautiful, nervous girls. However we got there, I found myself in a wet bathrobe in a hospital corridor asking God to spare my baby brother.

Next time... last call for snapdragons

RADICAL PRUNINGS

NOVEMBER 16

Gardening Advice by Mertensia Corydalis

HEAVEN DELAYED

Dear Readers,

The first time I heard Artie's disembodied voice. I was making a little pot of coffee. It was so startling, in the dim light of the early morning kitchen, that I had to steady myself for a moment. A rustle of static. Then: "I've got this craving. *Fraises des bois* with just a *soupçon* of really, really good balsamic vinegar. The syrupy kind that comes in little bottles. Hello? Is anybody there?"

"Go back to sleep, Artie, and dream on. *Fraises des bois* in Hamford? In November, no less? Get real."

I've had an intercom system installed, connecting the kitchen, the domain of my housekeeper, Erma Rhumtopf, and Artie's guest room, where he is recovering from his arterial blockage. He knows, and I know, that as soon as Maman arrives she will be on the phone, *tout de suite*, to Fauchon's ordering *fraises des bois* and balsamico, air express.

Artie is not the only unseasonable berrybrain. From this week's mailbag:

Q. Dear Miss Corydalis, this past spring I planted a small strawberry patch. I even got a few berries out of it. Actually, my dog Mr. Pepys got to the berries before me. Should I mulch the plants? Can I use leaves? —*Austen, Hamford*

A. Well, "Austen," you've certainly waited long enough. We've already had a hard freeze here in Hamford and in most areas of Zone 5. I hope you've kept that berry patch watered and weeded all summer. Leaves are not a suitable mulch for strawberries. Whole or chopped, they compact when wet and are too heavy for your berry plants. Apply three or four inches of loose straw over your plants. In late March begin to check for new growth emerging from the crowns. At this point remove the straw and use it in between the rows as a weed retardant. The most important requirement of your berry patch is very good drainage. Otherwise, plants with their roots sitting in wet soil are very likely to be done in by extreme cold. This is why we recommend planting in raised rows, with the runners removed as they creep into the aisles. If you have to replant the bed in the spring (this time, plant enough for both you and Mr. Pepys), I hope you will be more vigilant about mulching next autumn. After all, maintaining a garden requires prying oneself from the television set from time to time and facing the elements. One of my earliest memories of Artie—I must have been about four years old and Artie could barely walk—was of him plucking every strawberry, ripe or not, in Maman's garden, until his sand pail was overflowing and stashing the pile behind the gooseberry bushes. The imperious Little Me shrieked, "That's it! I'm telling Maman!"

The evidence on his chubby cheeks gave him away, but as usual, the cheeks were washed and kissed, and the whole episode was recounted at the dinner table under the category of "Adorable Things l'Enfant Artur Did Today." I'm certain that if my dollhouse father (cleverly named "Father" by me) had owned a safe with the world's tiniest coin collection, Artie would have slithered into my room while I slept and had the treasure fenced before morning recess at school.

His wings pinioned for the moment, Artie is amusing himself with his own Paul Newman film festival. On the way to the airport to greet Maman, who is coming to take charge of Artie's convalescence, I dropped off *The Color of Money*, *The Sting*, and *The Hustler* at the video store and rented *Cool Hand Luke* and *Sweet Bird of Youth*.

Maman's sling-back stiletto heels tip-tap on the tile floor at the airport (the rest of us would have feet swollen to the size of footballs after a transatlantic flight). She looks smart and trim in her Chanel pantsuit (a second marriage to an investment banker, who unfortunately succumbed to a heart attack while at his post at Crédit Lyonnaise, greatly expanded Maman's shopping capacity), and her hair is dyed dark gold. Last year she was a strawberry blond. With her opalescent green eyes and a just-got-out-of-bed voice with that little rasp, attributes which were passed on to Artie, not to me, she's as stunning as ever.

After the maternal embrace, she holds out my hands. "Mertensia! We are so busy with our books and lectures, we don't have time for salon manicures?" Suddenly the nearly two dozen garden books, the magazine columns, this newsletter, the Web site, all of it, falls away, and I am standing at the kitchen door in my coveralls, after tagging along behind Señor Delgado all day in the garden, and my fingernails are being inspected before I can join Artie for milk and *pain au chocolat*.

In the car, Maman chatters away about her life in Paris. Do you know we have *La Mode Gracieux* on the television? The housewives are crazy over l'Anglais, your Norton."

"He's not my Norton anymore, Maman. He's Delphine Doyle's Norton. Thank God." Another car popped into my lane with no signal. I gave the driver a blast of my horn. Even an innocent little drive in the car is perilous these days.

Maman reached over and patted my arm. "My poor Mertensia. Not to have a long and happy marriage like your Papa and me. Is there no man on the horizon?"

"I'm busy, Mother. I'm very, very busy."

Maman is crazy about Tran's special arrangement for the holidays—an allée of potted Norfolk pines spangled with tiny glass icicles, glittery snowflakes scattered on the entry hall floor. On weekends, when he comes to do a few outdoor chores and tend to my houseplants, Tran has been visiting Artie. He feels responsible for nearly killing my brother. Artie is teaching him card tricks. Not the kind of card tricks that will make you a sensation at your twelfth birthday party, but the kind that can land you in a hospital emergency room. Phoebe Denver, the director of the Metro Botanical Conservatory, has hired him away from me for the winter. This year, I fear he might not return in the spring.

I soon find Maman and Tran in the solarium. He is holding her hand as he discusses each of my orchids with her in a patois of English, French, and Vietnamese. Maman spent the late thirties in Saigon, a mystery period in her life. I once overheard Tante Martine talking about how Laurette ran off as a teenager with a French military officer to Indochine. But this was never spoken of in our house. They burst into laughter, Tran and Maman, and he presses her bony, freckled hand to his lips. She runs the back of her fingers over the smoothness of his cheek. It is a liberty taken that I cannot bear to watch. I head for the kitchen to make an American-style meat terrine for dinner. I will need to crush some old dried bread crusts under a rolling pin for the recipe.

After Tran had gone outside to turn the compost and rake up a few straggling leaves, the rigors of travel finally caught up with Maman. I found her fallen asleep in a chaise in the solarium. In the last blaze of light before sundown, her face was a graying ivory, rouged at the cheeks. With her eyes shut and her face expressionless and immobile, the red lips fallen open, I saw something I did not want to see.

Next time … don't go lightly on holly—it's the berries!

WINTER

Easy to fix, easy

efficiency

DARL...
AUTO...
...FUM
KILLS ALL PES...

...T'N. (15 min.). OUR WORKS ADJOI...

...E OF GREENHOUSE

ENI...

9 F' SMOKE PIPE

...rh reputation of this Boiler

No. 2 siz...

...e reco...
...eating A...
...pes on t...
...hous...
...side...

HAYWARDS BOILER

LIST and I...

G. HAYWARD &
BROCKLEY ROAD, LOND...

...issus bulbs

Mr. N. K. Gould will lecture on "Some Observations on the Hot Water Treatment of Narcissus Bulbs" on Tuesday, January 24th, at 3-30 p.m., in the Lecture Room of the Royal Horticultural Society's New Hall

The installation of th... roughly, the same cost as whilst the running cost i... of air heating. It has rendering air heating unn... is heated by radiation an...

RADICAL PRUNINGS

DECEMBER 1

Gardening Advice by Mertensia Corydalis

WHAT WE DID LAST SUMMER

Dear Readers,

These days we are poring over seed and nursery catalogues and planning next year's garden. Before we get carried away, take the following letter into consideration:

Q: **Miss Mertensia, by now you should have a received a little gift of horseradish put up by my partner Bob. It's a one-of-a-kind, because I've taken measures to make sure there will be no crop next year. In the future, if you get any questions on garden matters from Bob, please redirect them to me. He's been "bitten by the bug," and is scouring the Internet for pickled okra recipes.**
—*Nelson, Mt. Ashford*

A: It wouldn't kill us, dearest Nelson, to reserve a little space in our garden for the novice or the misguided who are flawed by having a different point of view. But you can rest easy. I am too bored by the very idea of okra to bother researching its cultivation for your partner. However, since you can count on an abundant crop anyway, you might consider drying and spraying the okra pods with metallic paints to add to your wreaths.

The carton containing two dozen jars of horseradish, with fetching gingham tops, arrived in sound condition. My thanks to you and Bob for your generosity. Since I have the mixed blessing of being a single person, living alone under normal circumstances, who could not do justice to your gift while it is at its savory peak, I will share the bounty with my houseguests. Happy Holidays!

While browsing my library for reading material to interest Artie, something more nourishing than the empty calories of horse-racing and beach-volleyball periodicals brought to him by Officer Steve, I rediscovered a book which I had not opened in many years. It is the first edition of my father's now-classic *Modern Follies: Whimsical Architecture for the Contemporary Garden.* On the dust cover there is a photograph of our family: Father. Myself (I must have been about ten years old), a child-size rake in one hand, the other hand in Father's. Maman, her curly blond hair held back with a bandanna and her smile so pretty and compelling that it is difficult to look away from her face. Artie in front of her, in the circle of her arms. Our Shetland collie, Duke, lying in the cool grass. In the background, Father's own folly, a Japanese tea house, which became so dilapidated over the years that I had to have it torn down. I, Lady Ichiban, painted with Maman's rouge and red lipstick, wearing her castoff silk bathrobe and espadrille wedgies; and Dukie as Lord Kyoto, his great fur mantle girded with a paisley obi, were the sole celebrants of the tea ceremony.

Officer Steve now takes his afternoon tea breaks with Miss Vong and me, joining us in time for *Sorrow's Beacon*. I quite innocently commented to Astrid, who is home from China for the holidays, that I will be marrying off Miss Vong before my very own daughter. This led to a little tiff about how much distance there is between us, how I wish her career would lead her back to America. So, she is busying herself meeting old boyfriends (all of them married by now, of course) for drinks, comparing notes on Thailand with her Uncle Artie (I hope to God Astrid's Bangkok and Artie's Bangkok are two different cities), and culling her old wardrobe for the consignment shop.

At Miss Vong's urging ("Go see Uncle Artie, he's so fun!"), Officer Steve has been stopping in to visit our star convalescent. The visits always end with roaring laughter spilling down the stairs. "Uncle Artie tell dirty joke," Francine tells me. "Like what?" I ask. "I am not permitted to hear these stories, stories from Singapore card club," she responds. Well, at least so far, Officer Steve hasn't visited with a warrant in hand.

A dispute has broken out between Frau Rhumtopf and Maman over Artie's care, as well as over a myriad of housekeeping details (this having once been Maman's home). Mothers come for visits and leave, but a reliable housekeeper is hard to find. So I suggested that Maman help Astrid on the closet-cleaning project.

Today a gleaming minivan pulled up to my front door and discharged eight elderly women dressed in bejeweled holiday sweaters. The leader introduced herself as Nettie and the others her Waverly Dam Garden Club friends. "The moment we read about Artie's collapse in your newsletter …we've been driving since five a.m. Can we visit with him a little while?" Not a "We're so excited to meet you; will you sign our copies of your latest book?" They're my readers, after all. The stairs are creaking these days from the parade of visitors.

In the kitchen where Frau Rhumtopf and I were preparing a little refreshment for the Waverly Dam ladies, the intercom squawked. "Tennie, I forgot that Willa is diabetic. Do you have some fruit or something without refined sugar? And Judy is caffeine-sensitive. Can you do a decaf tea or coffee for her?" I could hear a chorus of chatter in the background and, "Oh, Helen needs a glass of water to take her pills, too.

Frau Rhumtopf and I set out the trays in Artie's room. Nettie dipped into a shopping bag and pulled out a videocassette. "We brought all the tapes we made on Artie's wonderful European garden tour last year. We had so much fun!" One of the women, who I swear could pass for a skinny Gertrude Stein, rummaged through the bag, "Start with Antwerp. That was the most interesting." "No, Seville. My favorite," Helen, of the glass of water, protested. "The best was obviously Edinburgh," countered Nettie, with a little edge to her voice. "Cotswolds!" "Bagatelle in Paris!" "Don't worry, Artie, we'll get to all of them." A tape was popped into the player and in a moment there were poses by the ladies in front of hornbeam hedges. Poses in front of fountains. A shot of Artie seated at a table under a Cinzano umbrella, sipping a glass of wine, staring into the distance with a pained expression on his face. Poses in ruins.

As I turned to leave the bedroom, Artie, a desperate look in his eyes, called out, "Tennie, would you remind me in about a half hour to take my afternoon nap? I'm just worn out from doing my exercises. Please?"

"Artie, you've forgotten. You did your exercises this morning. You need to sit up longer and be a little more active. We don't want fluid in our lungs." I slipped out the door. "Enjoy."

It was time for *Sorrow's Beacon*, anyway. Tamara has gone off to anxiety camp for coping lessons, and she is being impersonated and having her life with Dr. Michael appropriated by Tanya, her twin, whom we thought had been asphyxiated after a plummet into a snow-filled crevasse while on her skiing honeymoon last year. In all, it was a perfect afternoon.

Tip for the week: there is still time to protect your precious mature shrubs from the harsh, drying winds of winter. Treat your evergreen azaleas and rhododendrons with an antidesiccant spray and cloak them in burlap.

Next time… tie it up, tie it down—everything in its own good twine

RADICAL PRUNINGS

DECEMBER 14

Gardening Advice by Mertensia Corydalis

NO QUESTIONS ASKED

Dear Readers,

It was a day of pleasant surprises, beginning with a package delivery service which brought a very large carton to my door. It bore a West Coast address that was not known to me, but surely, I decided, the box was too large to be a bomb. (You can't be too careful these days—there could be a disgruntled reader, some anti-environmentalist out there who disagrees with my organic philosophy of gardening.) Removing layers upon layers of packing materials revealed my penjing, firmly seated in its pot, the branches bare, as they should be this time of year, the trunks of the miniature trees unbroken. A new and, dare I say, more expressive little fisherman mud figure was returned to his favorite spot on the river bank. Scraping away a speck of bark from one of the trees revealed a bright green interior. The trees were alive. There was a card, written in a hand I knew well. "Weep no more for willows. Love."

After lunch, Artie, Miss Vong, and I were summoned to Astrid's room for a fashion show of old gowns destined for the consignment shop. To the latest machine-generated Japanese pop music and Miss Vong's Phat Maudit recordings, all the high school and college dances, all the girlfriends' weddings, all the New Year's Eves, even a party for an engagement that lasted a month were revisited. Depressing enough, for me, that Astrid can still fit in a decade-old sequined tube top and taffeta skirt, but Maman can wear it as well. Giving their best runway entrances from the bathroom-cum-changing room, they circled the bed with that bouncing strut that models do, stopping in front of our chairs, hand on hip, striking a pose to the right, an attitude to the left, a pirouette. For the finale, they came out together, Astrid in her butter-yellow taffeta junior-prom gown, Maman in a pink organza bridesmaid dress. We gave them a standing ovation. Astrid and Maman collapsed on the bed in a rainbow sherbet heap of tulle and silk and bows and crinolines and dyed-to-match shoes, laughing until tears came.

The gowns were returned to hangers and loaded into the Buick Roadmaster, with Astrid at the wheel, Maman in the back seat amidst the froth chattering away about how much Hamford has lost its charm with all the ugly new shopping malls ("Experience the Old World, Experience Brittany Village," elicits a special snort of contempt from Maman), and me trying to assist Astrid with directions to the consignment shop. "Stay in this lane, darling. You'll be making a left turn."

From the back: "Look at that! One awful Burger-this and Burger-that after another. No wonder everyone is so fat!"

"Maman, there are McDonald's all over Paris," I pointed out.

"They're for *les touristes*. The ones who eat all their meals with their hands."

"Watch, dear, that car's going to stop right in front of you! I don't think he has brake lights."

"Mother, I see him. I've been behind him for three blocks."

"I could take you and Artur for walks in your carriage. The new parts of the city—there are no sidewalks. What are they thinking? Where do they take walks?"

"They don't walk. Ever. Astrid, you'd better get in the turning lane!"

"Oh for Christ's sake, Mother, if I can get to Beijing by myself, I can get to the east side of Hamford."

"Cherie, you are distracting Astrid."

It's time. Astrid, after scheduling me for an exfoliation program, is off to New York to receive the Medal of Achievement from Amelia Faye herself for making the Modern Girl line of teen cosmetics, including the cologne Impudent!, the number one seller in China.

Sometimes I wish she had selected a mission in life with more gravity than cosmetics, something not so transitory. "It's a landscape, the face," she said with a startling testiness in her voice when I dared once to express my concern. "It's all artifice. What's the difference between plucking your eyebrows and painting a black line on your lids and that little apricot tree you tortured into a heart-shaped espalier?"

It's time for Maman, as well. She misses her geriatric Minou. There are theatre tickets with Didier, Minou's equally ancient veterinarian who has built his practice around operating on old cats. This development (Maman and Didier) is a result of weekly allergy shots—the cat's, that is. There are luncheon dates, a hair appointment. And the doctor has pronounced Artie well enough to go on with his life. Before Artie leaves, I'm going to require him to leave a kidney on deposit to cover his telephone calls.

I began this issue by telling you that today was a day of pleasant surprises. The next surprise arrived by hired limousine. At the door is another Parisienne of a certain age, with hair dyed dark gold and blood-red lacquered nails (it must be a thing there this season). "Dorinda!" Maman cries and the two women cling in a long embrace. Then from over Maman's shoulder, Dorinda caught sight of Tran as he was leaving from his afternoon visit. *"Bon Dieu! C'est si beau!"*

"Mais, mon pauvre Artur," continued Dorinda, *"C'est tragique, non? Si jeune!"*

I have to explain at this point that Dorinda de Westphalie (as in Westphalia Brass Valve Works) is one of Artie's "benefactresses," if you know what I mean, and I'm sure you do. I immediately see an opportunity to further reduce my list of houseguests. You may be dazzled by all the computer billionaires, but don't forget that every water closet from Papeete to Paducah, be it in a submarine, a spaceship, or in a suburban split-level, relies on a Westphalia brass valve.

Tran only stops by a few hours a day now, to visit with

Artie, tend my orchids, and do a little puttering outdoors. He is working full time at his winter job at the Metro Botanical Conservatory. Madame la Directress of the Conservatory, Phoebe Denver, has promoted Tran to Assistant *Orchidacae* Manager, putting a few noses out of joint. In spite of her alleged budgetary constraints, Phoebe is always on the prowl for staff to fill a chasmal void in her tropical area. I hold my breath every winter when she tries to steal my garden assistant from me. He says he will be on television in the new orchid wing of the conservatory.

I retreat to my bedroom, where I turn on the television to watch the news story on the orchidarium, but I've missed it. On to Gracious Way Network (all Delphine, all the time). My friend Yvette, the Food Editor, and Delphine demonstrate how *confit d'oie* is made. It's incredibly complicated—what Frenchwoman would find time these days, with her busy career as a stockbroker or cashier at the hypermarket, to embark on such a project?—but they accomplish it all between two commercials for the Delphine Doyle Signature Line of kitchen gadgets. After the goose has been stewed in its own fat until it falls off the carcass and jammed into an earthenware crock, Delphine promises to show us how to monogram our own automobile tires, as well as a foolproof way to park so that the monograms are all in the correct position. Is it my imagination or are this year's episodes featuring Delphine a little more out of focus than last year's?

On a segment called "Winter's Bounty," Norton gives us a tour of their newly constructed walk-in root cellar. I'm impressed, but so many rutabagas and parsnips for just two middle-aged people? Maybe company is coming. Norton's discourse on root vegetables ends with him, dressed in a French peasant's smock and wearing wooden sabots on his feet, standing amidst the now-barren rows of their vast culinary garden, gray roiling snow clouds above. Millet couldn't have done a better job setting up the shot. But wait…isn't that spot of red in the distance Norton's new 12-cylinder Turbinado 750 convertible (no doubt, all four tires bearing his monogram: N.O.D.)?

As the closing credits of the "The Cultivated Way" program rolled up the screen, I fell into a deep, peaceful sleep.

Next time … barking up the right tree: sycamores for cortical color

RADICAL PRUNINGS

JANUARY 2

Gardening Advice by Mertensia Corydalis

REFLECTIONS

Dear Readers,

I have to admit it: I'm going to miss Artie. He is off this week to St. Martin with Maman's friend Dorinda. He seems terribly dejected for someone who's going to spend the holidays baking on the beach. "It's never going to be the same, Tennie," he told me over cups of herbal tea. "After the heart attack, I lost some days. When I came to, I was a middle-aged man." He jerked his thumb at the bedside table. "I'm a cardiac patient now. Cholesterol pills. Blood pressure pills. Some heart pill that costs seven bucks apiece. I'm okay with giving up cigars and steak, but this…" he pulled open the nice blue cashmere robe presented to him by the Waverly Dam Garden Club, revealing the neon red scar about eight inches long down the middle of his chest. "That'll impress the ladies, huh?"

I told him that one of my girlfriends' husbands had the same operation and he's back, good as new, running his insurance agency and still cheating on my friend, as he always has.

No consolation there. "You know, I'm forty-eight years old

and the only job I've ever had was the neighborhood *Wall Street Journal* route when I was eleven. I sold the route to you—you were always better at getting up early. I'm forty-eight years old and I'm homeless as those poor bastards with the shopping carts. Hell, I don't even own a car or have a telephone number. My talent is knowing who needs a houseguest. There's that piddling trust income from the old man's estate. The rest... whatever opportunity comes up. Mostly, I've had a hell of a good time."

"Why don't you come down to the islands for a while this winter, Tennie? Walk on the beach with me. Touch up your tan. Talk with me. Dorinda...these older ladies..." He let it go. "It was all my choice, you understand. I had my freedom."

I needed to return to my office downstairs, so I gathered up the teacups. "You'll always have a home here, Artie." I winced the moment I said that. "As long as you keep your hands off my plant collection."

Halfway down the stairs, I called back, "By the way, thank you for the penjing. It's lovely, as ever."

Now, a letter which expresses the concerns of too many of our readers:

Q. Miss Mertensia, my sisters, Etta and Marijean, and I have shared our home for over fifty years. Our old bones are giving out and it is difficult for us to keep up our pride and joy, the garden. Children in the neighborhood no long come to the door looking for odd jobs. We only see them in their sports outfits being driven off by their mothers after school. We don't know where to turn. If we don't find help soon, we're going to have to sell our home and move into a retirement community. —*Nelda, Wiltshire*

A. Dear Nelda, I know too well your anxiety. The garden here at Miltonhurst will soon be in a state of chaos. My garden assistant Tran has taken a full-time position at the Metro Botanical Conservatory and now that nightfall comes early, he can only help me on the weekends.

Finding competent help is a universal problem. It seems that anyone who can follow a fifteen-dollar yard-sale lawn mower is setting himself up in the landscaping business. I suggest that you place an ad in the campus newspaper at Wiltshire College for a horticulture student to help you. But be prepared to pay a reasonable wage. Hort students are in great demand by nurseries in the spring and summer. Take it from someone who came with high recommendations from her professors and who, in her youth, could lift her body weight in peat moss, not to mention having a famous landscape architect for a father—attributes which were not lost on ambitious, social-climbing fellow graduate students. But enough about ex-husbands. Let me know how this turns out.

Next time... senescence: perennial doesn't mean forever

RADICAL PRUNINGS

JANUARY 12

Gardening Advice by Mertensia Corydalis

OUR NEWEST AMERICAN

Dear Readers,

You will be pleased to learn that our Miss Vong passed her citizenship exam with flying colors. Overprepared, she could top most American high school students on the subject of government, at least until she forgets it all, like the rest of us do. Our little entourage gathered at the Federal Court House today to witness the swearing-in of Citizen Vong. In her brand-new prim navy blue dress with a red and white star-spangled scarf and her hair done up in a bun, Miss Vong had transformed herself into a girl any young man could take home to meet his Republican grandmother.

After the ceremony I hosted a bit of a party, a combination New Year's and Naturalization bash, complete with little flags and paper dragons. Everyone was there: Miss Vong's girlfriends from the nail salon, Tran's soccer friends, the soulful-eyed Mr. Binh (ex-boyfriend) from Hanoi Hut Grocery and Carry-out who wore himself to a frazzle primping the buffet items he had catered, even Lord Byron from next door, and of course, Officer Steve, positively glowing with pride.

Language and cuisine were transcended by a game of cards, hopefully with none of Tran's newly acquired techniques employed. I overheard Officer Steve ask Tran if he will be the next one to become a citizen. He shrugged his shoulders. "Don't know. Maybe I'll go to France. I have some friends there." At that moment your Miss Mertensia was at the sideboard cutting up a fancy cake. I dropped the silver cake slicer, and everyone turned to look.

"Do you speak French?" he was asked.

"A little bit. Enough."

"Oh yeah. Patti LaBelle French," Miss Vong laughed. *"Voulez-vous couchez avec moi?"*

Tran fired back something in Vietnamese, and there was a little exchange.

After most of the guests had departed and I began to clear the cake plates and champagne glasses, Miss Vong and Officer Steve, inspired by the voulez-vous, stole away to my pantry, surrounded by the rows of sparkling glasses of jelly and pickles, bundles of drying rosemary and thyme, and the sugary smells coming from cookie jars, for a congratulatory kiss. Citizen Vong, you are one of us now.

RADICAL PRUNINGS

JANUARY 31

Gardening Advice by Mertensia Corydalis

THE ORCHIDARIUM

Dear Readers,

The Metro Botanical Conservatory has an ambitious new exhibition. Our locally based transmission-shop tycoon has financed the addition of a magnificent orchidarium. There were months of diplomatic negotiations (not to mention irate letters to the editor of the *Hamford Cornet,* mostly written by me) to avoid the name Shifty King Orchidarium; in the end the board compromised with the Harley Crampton Orchidarium. Having personally visited many native orchid habitats around the world, I am usually left cold by a conservatory's artificial boulders, fiberglass tree trunks, and pots barely disguised by tufts of Spanish moss, but Metro's new installation impressed even this jaded horticulturalist. Most of the specimens are clones of tissue culture, grown in flasks, but many have been collected (with permits, we hope) in the wild, wrenched from trees and forest floors in Brazil, Vietnam, Thailand, and Florida, and transplanted to this new glass-domed space, breathing a new kind of machine-generated and -conditioned air, mechanically misted on a schedule determined by a complex computer program.

It is a glittering debut party, with tiny candles tucked amidst the profusion of blooms. I've got on a new black velvet dinner suit, with a longish skirt slit up to the knee. I'm wearing Grandmother Corydalis's baroque black pearl-drop earrings with little diamonds. Besides being on the illustrated lecture schedule (bletillas—the hardy orchids native to western China), I am sort of a celebrity in Hamford garden circles. The Conservatory has required its orchidarium staff to wear Hawaiian shirts (something Tran would never wear, given a choice), but just for tonight they are in black tie with dark green tuxedo jackets and gold badges identifying them as orchidarium staff. Somewhat to my surprise, he looks entirely comfortable in evening clothes.

Tran is constantly being cornered by one woman or another, Mrs. Harley Crampton particularly, asking him every question they can dream up about orchid cultivation. He has become so easy with them, relaxed, with a hand in his pocket, letting his eyes stray from their expensive jewelry to their décolletage. I know these women. I designed most of their gardens. I know just what they want.

Tran has never seen me dressed this way. I want him to notice how I am dressed. I want him to think of me in a different way because of how I am dressed.

I want.

I am wanting.

Now Tran and I are chatting with the attorney I've hired to work on getting Phuong and the two children here. Tran is at once hopeful and terrified. What if it all falls through and they are denied permission to immigrate? What if they do immigrate? How will he ever support them all? I tell him it will work out. Phuong will learn English. She will continue being a nurse. It will work out.

The orchidarium is a large space, but the narrow paths dividing it by climatic zones, the humidity level, and the kaleidoscope of vivid colors make it feel close, almost stifling. I want a breath of cold winter air.

There are slides that flash on my screen:

Tran walking around a kitchen with a morning mug of coffee. "Why did you spend so much on groceries?"

Phuong: "Why are baguettes so hard to get here? Why do they cost so much?"

I close my eyes and move on to another slide in the carousel.

They have private jokes in bed as all couples do.

Another slide, quickly.

She is going crazy in the apartment. It is at least as large as her mother's home, with better plumbing, too, but it's cold outside in Hamford. Francine takes her to buy cold weather clothes. She has never owned a heavy coat in her life. She dreads the cold outside. She doesn't know how to dress her children.

Another slide. She can't understand what they are saying on television. She can't even read a newspaper.

Another slide. Why are all the fruits and vegetables at the

Vietnamese store a week old and preserved on ice? Why are there no markets with old women and their baskets of scallions and shallots, spice vendors with their intricate brass scales, so you need only buy a little paper packet of the freshest cinnamon? She notices that at the Vietnamese store, the teenagers who work there on weekends can barely speak their parents' language. Will that happen to her children?

Another slide. Pham is almost old enough for school. How will she tell the teacher that he has been spoiled rotten, the object of all her love and passion, that he is artistic like his father, and that if he doesn't have a long nap in the afternoon, he is a monster at dinner? She wants.

I want. I want the baby girl with wild black hair shooting from her head (we have photos now and a menacing little drawing by Pham). I want to feel her tiny hand cling to one of my fingers. There is a fire in her bright, dark eyes.

She is another Miss Vong about to be launched into the world. I want to be invited to her teddy-bear tea parties and buy her first pair of ballet slippers and give her a dollhouse so she can create a whole, better world of her own.

I am wanting. There is a children's science museum in Hamford where I used to take Astrid when she was a child. I understand it is even better now. I want to visit the science museum with Pham and Lilly. I want to make a big Christmas for them.

I want. I want.

Next time... red-twigged shrubs: the fires of winter

RADICAL PRUNINGS

Gardening Advice by Mertensia Corydalis

SPRING HOPES ETERNAL

Dear Readers,

Spring is just a snowmelt or two away and already we are itching to get to work in the garden. We have been dreaming all winter—for most of us the dreams exceed the reality that follows; no matter. I have been dreaming of a book to introduce young sprouts to the pleasures of gardening and will dedicate my efforts this year to coming up with some great projects for you to share with your children. Some of the happiest days of my life were spent gardening with my very own Astrid. While we admit to a tinge of disappointment that she did not carry on the family preoccupation, surely the early lessons about color and composition, about enhancing Nature, were not lost on her.

Unfortunately, some readers, like our friend Gene, whose letter follows, have spent a long winter's night dreaming about all the wrong things.

Q. Dear Miss Mertensia, just before a recent heavy snow, I noticed some bare spots in my lawn. I know that lawn like the back of my hand and can pinpoint the exact location of the spots under the snow. I called the ChemVelvet lawn service this morning. That was a waste of time. In spite of my contract with them, they refuse to send a technician out when the lawn is covered. What a bunch of wussies! Anyway, I noticed that the garden center here has BlastoGreen combination seed and starter fertilizer granules on preseason sale. Can I just broadcast the product on top of the snow? Am I right that, as the snow melts, the seed and granules will settle into the moist soil and be ready to germinate the moment the ground thaws a little? I'd appreciate a speedy reply as a warm spell is forecast for next week. —*Gene, Vista Verde*

A. Gene, you've been overcome by urea vapors from the BlastoGreen granules. Instead of fretting over a bald spot here and there, the winter months are better spent bringing armloads of gardening books home from the library (except my books, which you are encouraged to actually purchase), inspiring you to redirect your efforts and discover plant specimens more worthy of your obsessive disposition.

This is the perfect opportunity to put my readers on notice. Miss Vong has her instructions: There will be absolutely no lawn-care questions in the coming gardening season.

At least Gene, like the rest of us, has been haunting the garden stores for something, anything, to start growing—seeds for a new variety of sweet pea; a basket of shockingly blue pansies; a dwarfed but mighty little golden conifer—perhaps a whole trough of miniature conifers; a new bed devoted entirely to red raspberries that, warm from the bush, will melt in your mouth before you can ever get them to the kitchen.

No trip to the garden store is complete for me without popping into the greenhouse to look over the new arrivals, always hoping to find that one specimen which accidentally slipped into a shipment of otherwise unremarkable plant material. That is just what happened on a recent shopping expedition. I found just what I had been looking for. But so did another.

We circled the benches, nervously eyeing each other. He, a bit older than I, of sturdy build and ruddy complexion, hair gone silver. We pretended not to be aware of each other, inspecting this, fingering that. He may have been attracted to form; perhaps he was intoxicated by perfume, or it might have been an uncontrollable surge of lust brought on by the sultry atmosphere of the greenhouse. Whatever motivated his wanton, irrational behavior, without warning I found his hand firmly on my zygopetalum.

"Sir, remove your hand from my zygopetalum immediately!" I commanded.

"Madame, I saw it first." While he spoke perfectly acceptable English, there was an accent I could not quite place. Not German. It might have been Dutch.

"The hell you did! This zygopetalum is mine." I tried to wrench the pot from his hands, but his grip was unyielding. Just as he was about to snatch it up from the bench, I swung my purse down on his arms with all the force I could muster. Readers, you know your Miss Mertensia is not of a violent nature, but a woman must defend her most sweetly-scented fragile prizes.

The Dutchman, as I'll call him since I never learned his name, stepped back, rubbing his arm. "Madame, you are a harpy." His icy blue eyes regarded me with loathing. Well, one of his eyes, anyway. The other seemed to be lifeless, as though from an injury.

"Sir, you are a beast."

"Ah, have the *godverdomde* orchid then. I should sue you or have you arrested." He stalked out of the greenhouse muttering what I'm sure are very nasty words in Dutch. I hoped I would never see that hateful man again!

I clutched the pot to my breast, the freckled brown and blue blooms bobbing proudly on the end of the flower spike, the scent intensified by agitation, and marched triumphantly to the cashier.

My new pet secured next to me on the front seat of the Buick Roadmaster, I began to wonder how the Dutchman lost the use of his eye. No doubt it resulted from his aggressive nature, especially toward the defenseless. And I noticed that his arms, which he accused me of injuring, appeared strong beneath their wisps of white fur, not the arms of a limp orchid connoisseur, but arms that have broken soil and built stone walls. To glance over, in the garden, to brush against an arm, just to barely brush the hairs, tiny crumbs of good garden dirt suspended in those hairs, that would be a reassuring thing.

Dear Readers, a woman has to fix her mind on what she wants and let nothing stand in her way.

—*Mertensia Corydalis*

ABOUT THE AUTHOR

Bonnie Thomas Abbott is a licensed humor essayist whose earliest flings at fiction included lip-syncing "I'm a Little Teapot" (it compromised her dignity), daydreaming in class (Mr. Thomas informed the second-grade teacher that daydreaming was just fine with him), and a neatly printed short story titled "It Took Guts," inspired by her big brother's tour of duty in the Korean War.

Ms. Abbott grew up on an organic hobby farm where heated dinner table discussions involved points of grammar and English usage. Genetically inclined to the pursuit of growing things, it was inevitable that this, her first novel, would dispense gardening tips along with gossipy updates on the household of horticulturist Miss Mertensia Corydalis.

Other work of hers appears in *Mirth of a Nation*, *101 Damnations*, and other fine publications. She lives in Columbus, Ohio.